The Land of the Blessed Virgin
Sketches and Impressions in Andalusia

W. Somerset Maugham

The Land of the Blessed Virgin: Sketches and Impressions in Andalusia

The present edition is a reproduction of previous publication of this classic work. Minor typographical errors may have been corrected without note, however, for an authentic reading experience the spelling, punctuation, and capitalization have been retained from the original text.

ISBN: 978-1-61895-971-3

Contents

I

The Spirit of Andalusia

After one has left a country it is interesting to collect together the emotions it has given in an effort to define its particular character. And with Andalusia the attempt is especially fascinating, for it is a land of contrasts in which work upon one another, diversely, a hundred influences.

In London now, as I write, the rain of an English April pours down; the sky is leaden and cold, the houses in front of me are almost terrible in their monotonous greyness, the slate roofs are shining with the wet. Now and again people pass: a woman of the slums in a dirty apron, her head wrapped in a grey shawl; two girls in waterproofs, trim and alert notwithstanding the inclement weather, one with a music-case under her arm. A train arrives at an underground station and a score of city folk cross my window, sheltered behind their umbrellas; and two or three groups of workmen, silently, smoking short pipes: they walk with a dull, heavy tramp, with the gait of strong men who are very tired. Still the rain pours down unceasing.

And I think of Andalusia. My mind is suddenly ablaze with its sunshine, with its opulent colour, luminous and soft; I think of the cities, the white cities bathed in light; of the desolate wastes of sand, with their dwarf palms, the broom in flower. And in my ears I hear the twang of the guitar, the rhythmical clapping of hands and the castanets, as two girls dance in the sunlight on a holiday. I see the crowds going to the bull-fight, intensely living, many-coloured. And a thousand scents are wafted across my memory; I remember the cloudless nights, the silence of sleeping towns, and the silence of desert country; I remember old whitewashed taverns, and the perfumed wines of Malaga, of Jerez, and of Manzanilla. (The rain pours down without stay in oblique long lines, the light is quickly failing, the street is sad and very cheerless.) I feel on my shoulder the touch of dainty hands, of little hands with tapering fingers, and on my mouth the kisses of red lips, and I hear a joyous laugh. I

1

remember the voice that bade me farewell that last night in Seville, and the gleam of dark eyes and dark hair at the foot of the stairs, as I looked back from the gate. 'Feliz viage, mi Inglesito.'

It was not love I felt for you, Rosarito; I wish it had been; but now far away, in the rain, I fancy, (oh no, not that I am at last in love,) but perhaps that I am just faintly enamoured—of your recollection.

But these are all Spanish things, and more than half one's impressions of Andalusia are connected with the Moors. Not only did they make exquisite buildings, they moulded a whole people to their likeness; the Andalusian character is rich with Oriental traits; the houses, the mode of life, the very atmosphere is Moorish rather than Christian; to this day the peasant at his plough sings the same quavering lament that sang the Moor. And it is to the invaders that Spain as a country owes the magnificence of its golden age: it was contact with them that gave the Spaniards cultivation; it was the conflict of seven hundred years that made them the best soldiers in Europe, and masters of half the world. The long struggle caused that tension of spirit which led to the adventurous descent upon America, teaching recklessness of life and the fascination of unknown dangers; and it caused their downfall as it had caused their rise, for the religious element in the racial war occasioned the most cruel bigotry that has existed on the face of the earth, so that the victors suffered as terribly as the vanquished. The Moors, hounded out of Spain, took with them their arts and handicrafts—as the Huguenots from France after the revocation of the Edict of Nantes—and though for a while the light of Spain burnt very brightly, the light borrowed from Moordom, the oil jar was broken and the lamp flickered out.

In most countries there is one person in particular who seems to typify the race, whose works are the synthesis, as it were, of an entire people. Bernini expressed in this manner a whole age of Italian society; and even now his spirit haunts you as you read the gorgeous sins of Roman noblemen in the pages of Gabriele d'Annunzio. And Murillo, though the expert not unjustly from their special point of view, see in him but a mediocre artist, in the same way is the very quintessence of Southern Spain. Wielders of the brush, occupied chiefly with technique, are apt to discern little in an old master, save the craftsman; yet art is no more than a link in the chain of life and cannot be sharply sundered from the civilisation of which it is an outcome: even Velasquez, sans peer, sans parallel, throws a curious light on the world of his day, and the cleverest painters would find their knowledge and understanding of that great genius the fuller if they were acquainted with the plays of Lope de la Vega and the satires of Quevedo. Notwithstanding Murillo's obvious faults, as you walk through the museum at Seville all Andalusia appears before you. Nothing could be more characteristic than the religious feeling of the many pictures, than the exuberant fancy and utter lack of idealisation: in the contrast between a Holy Family by Murillo and one by Perugino is all the difference between Spain and Italy. Murillo's Virgin is a peasant girl such as you may see in any village round Seville on a feast-day; her emotions are purely human, and in her face is nothing more than the intense love of a mother for her child. But the Italian shows a creature not of earth, an angelic maid with almond eyes, oval of face: she has a strange air of unrealness, for her body is not of human flesh and blood, and she is linked with mankind only by an infinite sadness; she seems to see already the Dolorous Way, and her eyes are heavy with countless unwept tears.

One picture especially, that which the painter himself thought his best work, Saint Thomas of Villanueva distributing Alms, to my mind offers the entire impression of that full life of Andalusia. In the splendour of mitre and of pastoral staff, in the sober magnificence of architecture, is all the opulence of the Catholic Church; in the worn, patient, ascetic face of the saint is the mystic, fervid piety which distinguished so wonderfully the warlike and barbarous Spain of the sixteenth century; and lastly, in the beggars covered with sores, pale, starving, with their malodorous rags, you feel strangely the swarming poverty of the vast population, downtrodden and vivacious, which you read of in the picaresque novels of a later day. And these same characteristics, the deep religious feeling, the splendour, the poverty, the extreme sense of vigorous life, the discerning may find even now among the Andalusians for all the modern modes with which, as with coats of London and bonnets of Paris, they have sought to liken themselves to the rest of Europe.

And the colours of Murillo's palette are the typical colours of Andalusia, rich, hot, and deep—again contrasting with the enamelled brilliance of the Umbrians. He seems to have charged his brush with the very light and atmosphere of Seville; the country bathed in the splendour of an August sun has just the luminous character, the haziness of contour, which characterise the paintings of Murillo's latest manner. They say he adopted the style termed vaporoso for greater rapidity of execution, but he cannot have lived all his life in that radiant atmosphere without being impregnated with it. In Andalusia there is a quality of the air which gives all things a limpid, brilliant softness, the sea of gold poured out upon them voluptuously rounds away their outlines; and one can well imagine that the master deemed it the culmination of his art when he painted with the same aureate effulgence, when he put on canvas those gorgeous tints and that exquisite mellowness.

II

The Churches of Ronda

That necessity of realism which is, perhaps, the most conspicuous of Spanish traits, shows itself nowhere more obviously than in matters religious. It is a very listless emotion that is satisfied with the shadow of the ideal; and the belief of the Andaluz is an intensely living thing, into which he throws himself with a vehemence that requires the nude and brutal fact. His saints must be fashioned after his own likeness, for he has small power of make-believe, and needs all manner of substantial accessories to establish his faith. But then he treats the images as living persons, and it never occurs to him to pray to the Saint in Paradise while kneeling before his presentment upon earth. The Spanish girl at the altar of Mater Dolorosa prays to a veritable woman, able to speak if so she wills, able to descend from the golden shrine to comfort the devout worshipper. To her nothing is more real than these Madonnas, with their dark eyes and their abundant hair: Maria del Pilar, who is Mary of the Fountain, Maria del Rosario, who is Mary of the Rosary, Maria de los Dolores, Maria del Carmen, Maria de los Angeles. And they wear magnificent gowns of brocade and of cloth-of-gold, mantles heavily embroidered, shoes, rings on their fingers, rich jewels about their necks.

In a little town like Ronda, so entirely apart from the world, poverty-stricken, this desire for realism makes a curiously strong impression. The churches, coated with whitewash, are squalid, cold and depressing; and at first sight the row of images looks nothing more than a somewhat vulgar exhibition of wax-work. But presently, as I lingered, the very poverty of it all touched me; and forgetting the grotesqueness, I perceived that some of the saints in their elaborate dresses were quite charming and graceful. In the church of Santa Maria la Mayor was a Saint Catherine in rich habiliments of red brocade, with a white mantilla arranged as only a Spanish woman could arrange it. She might have been a young gentlewoman of fifty years back when costume was gayer than nowadays, arrayed for a fashionable wedding or for a bull-fight. And in another church I saw a youthful Saint in priest's robes, a cassock of black silk and a short surplice of exquisite lace; he held a bunch of lilies in his hand and looked very gently, his lips almost trembling to a smile. One can imagine that not to them would come the suppliant with a heavy despair, they would be merely pained at their helplessness before the tears of the grief that kills and the woe of mothers sorrowing for their sons. But when the black-eyed maiden knelt before the priest, courtly and debonair, begging him to send a husband quickly, his lips surely would control themselves no longer, and his smile would set the damsel's cheek a-blushing. And if a youth knelt before Saint Catherine in her dainty mantilla, and vowed his heart was breaking because his love gave him stony glances, she would look very graciously upon him, so that his courage was restored, and he promised her a silver heart as lovers in Greece made votive offerings to Aphrodite.

At the Church of the Espirito Santo, in a little chapel behind one of the transept altars, I saw, through a huge rococo frame of gilded wood, a Maria de los Dolores that was almost terrifying in poignant realism. She wore a robe of black damask, which stood as if it were cast of bronze in heavy, austere folds, a velvet cloak decorated with the old lace known as rose point d'Espagne; and on her head a massive imperial diadem, and a golden aureole. Seven candles burned before her; and at vespers, when the church was nearly dark, they threw a cold, sharp light upon her countenance. Her eyes were in deep shadow, strangely mysterious, and they made the face, so small beneath the pompous crown, horribly life-like: you could not see the tears, but you felt they were eyes which would never cease from weeping.

I suppose it was all tawdry and vulgar and common, but a woman knelt in front of the Mother of Sorrows, praying, a poor woman in a ragged shawl; I heard a sob, and saw that she was weeping; she sought to restrain herself and in the effort a tremor passed through her body, and she drew the shawl more closely round her.

I walked away, and came presently to the most cruel of all these images. It was a Pietà. The Mother held on her knees the dead Son, looking in His face, and it was a ghastly contrast between her royal array and His naked body. She, too, wore the imperial crown, with its golden aureole, and her cloak was of damask embroidered with heavy gold. Her hair fell in curling abundance about her breast, and the sacristan told me it was the hair of a lady who had lost her

6

husband and her only son. But the dead Christ was terrible, His face half hidden by the long straight hair, long as a woman's, and His body thin and all discoloured: from the wounds thick blood poured out, and their edges were swollen and red; the broken knees, the feet and hands, were purple and green with the beginning of putrefaction.

III

Ronda

Ronda is set deep among the mountains between Algeciras and Seville; they hem it in on all sides, and it straggles up and down little hills, timidly, as though its presence were an affront to the wild rocks around it. The houses are huddled against the churches, which look like portly hens squatting with ruffled feathers, while their chicks, for warmth, press up against them. It is very cold in Ronda. I saw it first quite early: over the town hung a grey mist shining in the sunlight, and the mountains, opalescent in the morning glow, were so luminous that they seemed hardly solid; they looked as if one could walk through them. The people, covering their mouths in dread of a pulmonia, hastened by, closely muffled in long cloaks. As I passed the open doors I saw them standing round the brasero, warming themselves; for fireplaces are unknown to Andalusia, the only means of heat being the copa, a round brass dish in which is placed burning charcoal.

The height and the cold give Ronda a character which reminds one of Northern Spain; the roofs are quite steep, the houses low and small, built for warmth rather than, as in the rest of Andalusia, for coolness.

But the whitewash and the barred windows with their wooden lattice-work, remind you that you are in Moorish country, in the very heart of it; and Ronda, indeed, figures in chronicles and in old ballads as a stronghold of the invaders. The temperature affects the habits of the people, even their appearance: there is no lounging about the squares or at the doors of wine-shops, the streets are deserted and their great breadth makes the emptiness more apparent. The first setters out of the town had no need to make the ways narrow for the sake of shade, and they are, in fact, so broad that the houses on either side might be laid on their faces, and there would still be room for the rapid stream which hurries down the middle.

The conformation of a Spanish town, even though it lack museums and fine buildings, gives it an interest beyond that of most

European places. The Moorish design is always evident. That wise people laid out the streets as was most convenient, tortuous and narrow at Cordova or broad as a king's highway in Ronda. The Moors stayed their time, and their hour struck, and they went; the houses had fallen to decay and been more than once rebuilt. The Christians returned and Mahomet fled before the Saints; (it was no shame since they grossly out-numbered him;) the mosque was made a church, and the houses as they fell were built again, but on the same foundations and in the same way. The streets have remained as the Moors left them, the houses still are built round little courtyards—the patio—as the Moors built them; and the windows are barred and latticed as of old, the better to protect beauty whose dark eyes flash too meaningly at wandering strangers, whose red lips are over ready to break into a smile for the peace of an absent husband.

After the busy clamour of Gibraltar, that ant-nest of a hundred nationalities, Ronda impresses you by its peculiar silence. The lack of sound is the more noticeable in the frosty clearness of the atmosphere, and is only emphasised by an occasional cry that floats, from some vast distance, along the air. The coldness, too, has pinched the features of the people, and they seem to grow old even earlier than in the rest of Andalusia. Strapping fellows of thirty with slim figures and a youthful air have the faces of elderly men, and their skin is hard, stained and furrowed. The women, ageing as rapidly, have no gaiety. If Spanish girls have frequently a beautiful youth, their age too often is atrocious: it is inconceivable that a handsome woman should become so fearful a hag; the luxuriant hair is lost, and she takes no pains to conceal her grey baldness, the eye loses its light, the enchanting down of the upper lip turns to a bristly moustache; the features harden, grow coarse and vulgar; and the countenance assumes a rapacious expression, so that she appears a bird of prey; and her strident voice is like the shriek of vultures. It is easily comprehensible that the Spanish stage should have taken the old woman as one of its most constant, characteristic types. But in Ronda even the girls have a weary look, as though life were not so easy a matter as in warmer places, or as the good God intended; and they seem to suffer from the brevity of youth, which is no sooner come than gone. They walk inertly, clothed in sombre colours, their hair not elaborately arranged as would have it the poorest cigarette-girl, but merely knotted, without the flower which the Sevillan is popularly said to insist upon even at the cost of a dinner. And when they go out the grey shawls they wrap about their heads add to their unattractiveness.

9

IV

The Swineherd

But if Ronda itself is a somewhat dull and unsympathetic place with nothing more for the edification of the visitor than a melodramatic chasm, the surrounding country is worthy the most extravagant epithets. The mountains have the gloomy barrenness, the slate-grey colour of volcanic ranges; they encircle the town in a gigantic amphitheatre, rugged and overbearing like Titans turned to stone. They seem, indeed, to wear a sombre insolence of demeanour as though the aspect of human kind moved them to lofty contempt. And in their magnificent desolation they offer a fit environment for the exploits of Byronic heroes. The handsome villain of romance, seductive by the complexity of his emotions, by the persistence of his mysterious grief, would find himself in that theatrical scene most thoroughly at home; nor did Prosper Mérimée fail to seize the opportunity, for the mountains of Ronda were the very hunting-ground of Don Josè, who lost his soul for Carmen. But as a matter of history they were likewise the haunts of brigands in flesh and blood—malefactors in the past had that sense of the picturesque which now is vested in the amateur photographer—and this particular district was as dangerous to the travelling merchant as any in Spain.

The environs of Ronda are barren and unfertile, the olive groves bear little fruit. I wandered through the lonely country, towards the mountains; the day was overcast and the clouds hung sluggishly overhead. As I walked, suddenly I heard a melancholy voice singing a peasant song, a malagueña. I paused to listen, but the sadness was almost unendurable; and it went on interminably, wailing through the air with the insistent monotony of its Moorish origin. I struck into the olives to find the singer and met a swineherd, guarding a dozen brown pigs, a youth thin of face, with dark eyes, clothed in undressed sheep-skins; and the brown wool gave him a singular appearance of community with the earth about him. He stood among the trees like a wild creature, more beast than man, and the lank, busy pigs burrowed around him, running to and fro, with little squeals. He ceased his song when I approached and looked up timidly. I spoke to him but he made no answer, I offered a cigarette but he shook his head.

I went my way, and at first the road was not quite solitary. Two men passed me on donkeys. 'Vaya Usted con Dios!' they cried—'Go you with God': it is the commonest greeting in Spain, and the most charming; the roughest peasant calls it as you meet him. A dozen grey asses went towards Ronda, one after the other, their panniers filled with stones; they walked with hanging heads, resigned to all their pain. But when at last I came into the mountains the loneliness was terrible. Not even the olive grew on those dark masses of rock, windswept and sterile; there was not a hut nor a cottage to testify of man's existence, not even a path such as the wild things of the heights might use. All life, indeed, appeared incongruous with that overwhelming solitude.

Daylight was waning as I returned, but when I passed the olive-grove, where many hours before I had heard the malagueña, the same monotonous song still moaned along the air, carrying back my thoughts to the swineherd. I wondered what he thought of while he sang, whether the sad words brought him some dim emotion. How curious was the life he led! I suppose he had never travelled further than his native town; he could neither write nor read. Madrid to him was a city where the streets were paved with silver and the King's palace was of fine gold. He was born and grew to manhood and tended his swine, and some day he would marry and beget children, and at length die and return to the Mother of all things. It seemed to me that nowadays, when civilisation has become the mainstay of our lives, it is only with such beings as these that it is possible to realise the closeness of the tie between mankind and nature. To the poor herdsman still clung the soil; he was no foreign element in the scene, but as much part of it as the stunted olives, belonging to the earth intimately as the trees among which he stood, as the beasts he tended.

When I came near the town the sun was setting. In the west, tempestuous clouds were massed upon one another, and the sun shone blood-red above them; but as it sank they were riven asunder, and I saw a great furnace that lit up the whole sky. The mountains were purple, unreal as the painted mountains of a picture. The light was gone from the east, and there everything was chill and grey; the barren rocks looked so desolate that one shuddered with horror of

11

the cold. But the sun fell gold and red, and the rift in the clouds was a kingdom of gorgeous light; the earth and its petty inhabitants died away, and in the crimson flame I could almost see Lucifer standing in his glory, god-like and young; Lucifer in all majesty, surrounded by his court of archangels, Beelzebub, Belial, Moloch, Abaddon.

I had discovered in the morning, from the steeple of Santa Maria, a queer ruined church, and was oddly impressed by the bare façade, with the yawning apertures of empty windows. I went to it, but every entrance was bricked up save one, which had a door of rough boards fastened by a padlock; and in a neighbouring house I found an old man with a key. It was a spot of utter desolation; the roof had gone or had never been. The custodian could not tell whether the church was the wreck of an old building or a framework that had never been completed; the walls were falling to decay. Along the nave and in the chapels trees were growing, shrubs and rank weeds; it was curious the utter ruin in the midst of the populous town. Pigs ran hither and thither, feeding, with noisy grunts, as they burrowed about the crumbling altar.

The old man inquired whether I wished to buy the absolute uselessness of the place fascinated me. I asked the price. He looked me up and down, and seeing I was foreign, suggested a ridiculous sum. And while I amused myself with bargaining, I wondered what on earth one could do with a ruined church in Ronda. Half a dozen fantastic notions passed through my mind, but they were really too melodramatic.

And now when the sun had set I returned. Notwithstanding his suspicions, I induced the keeper to give me his key; he could not understand what I desired at such an hour in that solitary place, and asked if I wished to sleep there! But I calmed his fears with a peseta—money goes a long way in Spain—and went in alone. The pigs had been removed and all was silent. A few bats flitted to and fro quickly. The light fell away greyly, the cold descended on the ruin, and it became very strange and mysterious. Presently, the roofless chapels seemed to grow alive with weird invisible things, the rank weeds exhaled chill odours; and in the lonely silence a mass began. At the ruined altar ghostly priests officiated, passing quietly from side to side, with bows and genuflections. The bell tinkled as they raised an invisible host. Soon it became quite dark, and the moon shone through the great empty windows of the façade.

V

Medinat Az-Zahra

In what you divine rather than in what you see lies half the charm of Andalusia, in the suggestion of all manner of delicate antique things, in the vivid memory of past grandeur. The Moors have gone, but still they inhabit the land in spirit and not seldom in a spectral way seem to regain their old dominion. Often towards evening, as I rode through the desolate country, I thought I saw an half-naked Moor ploughing his field, urging the lazy oxen with a long goad. Often the Spaniard on his horse vanished, and I saw a Muslim knight riding in pride and glory, his velvet cloak bespattered with the gold initial of his lady, and her favour fluttering from his lance. Once near Granada, standing on a hill, I watched the blood-red sun set tempestuously over the plain; and presently in the distance the gnarled olive-trees seemed living beings, and I saw contending hosts, two ghostly armies silently battling with one another; I saw the flash of scimitars, and the gleam of standards, the whiteness of the turbans. They fought with horrible carnage, and the land was crimson with their blood. Then the sun fell below the horizon, and all again was still and lifeless.

And what can be more fascinating than that magic city of Az-Zahra, the wonder of its age, of which now not a stone remains? It was made to satisfy the whim of a concubine by a Sultan whose flamboyant passion moved him to displace mountains for the sake of his beloved; and the memory thereof is lost so completely that even its situation till lately was uncertain. Az-Zahra the Fairest said to Abd-er-Rahmān, her lord: 'Raise me a city that shall take my name and be mine.' The Khalif built at the foot of the mountain which is called the Hill of the Bride; but when at last the lady, from the great hall of the palace, gazed at the snow-white city contrasting with the dark mountain, she remarked: 'See, O Master! how beautiful this girl looks in the arms of yonder Ethiopian.' The jealous Khalif immediately commanded the removal of the offending hill; and when he was convinced the task was impossible, ordered that the oaks and other mountain trees which grew upon it

13

should be uprooted, and fig-trees and almonds planted in their stead.

Imagine the Hall of the Khalif, with walls of transparent and many-coloured marble, with roof of gold; on each side were eight doors fixed upon arches of ivory and ebony, ornamented with precious metals and with precious stones; and when the sun penetrated them, the reflection of its rays upon the roof and walls was sufficient to deprive the beholders of sight! In the centre was a great basin filled with quicksilver, and the Sultan, wishing to terrify a courtier, would cause the metal to be set in motion, whereupon the apartment would seem traversed by flashes of lightning, and all the company would fall a-trembling.

The old author tells of running streams and of limpid water, of stately buildings for the household guards, and magnificent palaces for the reception of high functionaries of state; of the thronging soldiers, pages, eunuchs, slaves, of all nations and of all religions, in sumptuous habiliments of silk and of brocade; of judges, theologians, and poets, walking with becoming gravity in the ample courts.... Alas! that poets now should rush through Fleet Street with unseemly haste, attired uncouthly in bowler hats and in preposterous tweeds!

From the celebrated legend of Roderick the Goth to that last scene when Boabdil handed the keys of Granada to King Ferdinand, the history of the Moorish occupation reads far more like romance than like sober fact. It is rich with every kind of passionate incident; it has all the strange vicissitudes of oriental history. What career could be more wonderful than that of Almanzor, who began life as a professional letter-writer, (a calling which you may still see exercised in the public places of Madrid or Seville,) and ended it as absolute ruler of an Empire! His charm of manner, his skill in flattery, the military genius which he developed when occasion called, his generosity and sense of justice, his love of literature and art, make him a figure to be contemplated with admiration; and when you add his utter lack of scruple, his selfishness, his ingratitude, his perfidy, you have a character complex enough to satisfy the most exacting.

Those who would read of these things may find an admirable account in Mr. Lane-Poole's Moors in Spain; but I cannot renounce the pleasure of giving one characteristic detail. After the death of

Abd-er-Rahmān, the builder of that magnificent city of Az-Zahra, a paper was found in his own handwriting, upon which he had noted those days in his long reign which had been free from all sorrow: they numbered fourteen. Sovereign lord of a country than which there is on earth none more delightful, his life had been of uninterrupted prosperity; success in peace and war attended him always; he possessed everything that it was possible for man to have. These are the observations of Al Makkary, the Arabic historian, when he narrates the incident:

O man of understanding! Wonder and observe the small portion of real happiness the world affords even in the most enviable position. Praise be given to Him, the Lord of eternal glory and everlasting empire! There is no God but He the Almighty, the Giver of Empire to whomsoever He pleases.

VI

The Mosque

But Cordova, from which Az-Zahra was about four miles distant, has visible delights that can vie with its neighbour's vanished pomp. I know nothing that can give a more poignant emotion than the interior of the mosque at Cordova; and yet I remember well the splendour of barbaric and oriental magnificence which was my first sight of St. Mark's at Venice, as I came abruptly from the darkness of an alley into the golden light of the Piazza. But to me at least the famous things of Italy, known from childhood in picture and in description, afford more than anything a joyful sense of recognition, a feeling as it were of home-coming, such as may hope to experience the devout Christian on entering upon his heritage in the Kingdom of Heaven. The mosque of Cordova is oriental and barbaric too; but I had never seen nor imagined anything in the least resembling it; there was no disillusionment possible, as too often in Italy, for the accounts I had read prepared me not at all for that overwhelming impression. It was so weird and strange, I felt myself transported suddenly to another world.

They were singing Vespers when I entered, and I heard the shrill voices of choristers crying the responses; it did not sound like Christian music. The mosque was dimly lit, the air heavy with incense; and I saw this forest of pillars, extending every way, as far as the eye could reach. It was mysterious and awe-inspiring as those enchanted forests of one's childhood in which huge trees grew in serried masses and where in cavernous darkness goblins and giants of the fairy-tales, wild beasts and monstrous shapes, lay in wait for the terrified traveller who had lost his way. I wandered, keeping the Christian chapels out of sight, trying to lose myself among the columns; and now and then gained views of horseshoe arches interlacing, decorated with Moorish tracery.

At length I came to the Mihrab, which is the Holy of Holies, the most exquisite as well as the most sacred part of the mosque. It is approached by a vestibule of which the roof is a miracle of grace, with mosaics that glow like precious stones, ultramarine, scarlet,

16

emerald, and gold. The arch between the chambers is ornamented with four pillars of coloured marble, and again with mosaic, the gold letters of an Arabic inscription forming on the deep sapphire of the background a decorative pattern. The Mihrab itself, which contained the famous Koran of Othman, has seven sides of white marble, and the roof is a huge shell cut from a single block.

I tried to picture to myself the mosque before the Christians laid their desecrating hands upon it. The floor was of coloured tiles, tiles such as may still be seen in the Alhambra of Granada and in the Alcazar at Seville. The columns are of marble, of porphyry and jasper; tradition says they came from Carthage, from pagan temples in France and Christian churches in Spain; they are slender and unadorned, they must have contrasted astonishingly with the roof of larch wood, all ablaze with gold and with vermilion.

There were three hundred chandeliers; and eight thousand lamps— cast of Christian bells—hung from the roof. The Arab writer tells of gold shining from the ceiling like fire, blazing like lightning when it darts across the clouds. The pulpit, wherein was kept the Koran, was of ivory and of exquisite woods, of ebony and sandal, of plantain, citron and aloe, fastened together with gold and silver nails and encrusted with priceless gems. It needed six Khalifs and Almanzor, the great Vizier, to complete the mosque of which Arab writers, with somewhat prosaic enthusiasm, said that 'in all the lands of Islam there was none of equal size, none more admirable in its workmanship, in its construction and durability.'

Then the Christians conquered Cordova, and the charming civilisation of the Moors was driven out by monks and priests and soldiers. First they built only chapels in the outermost aisles; but in a little while, to make room for a choir, they destroyed six rows of columns; and at last, when Master Martin Luther had rekindled Catholic piety, they set up a great church in the very middle of the mosque. The story of this vandalism is somewhat quaint, and one detail at least affords a suggestion that might prove useful in the present time; for the Town Council of Cordova menaced with death all who should assist in the work: one imagines that a similar threat from the Lord Mayor of London might have a salutary effect upon the restorers of Westminster Abbey or the decorators of St. Paul's. How very much more entertaining must have been the world when absolutism was the fashion and the preposterous method of universal suffrage had never been considered! But the Chapter, as those in power always are, was bent upon restoring, and induced Charles V. to give the necessary authority. The king, however, had not understood what they wished to do, and when later he visited Cordova and saw what had happened, he turned to the dignitaries who were pointing out the improvements and said: 'You have built what you or others might have built anywhere, but you have destroyed something that was unique in the world.' The words show a fine scorn; but as a warning to later generations it would have been more to the purpose to cut off a dozen priestly heads.

Yet oddly enough the Christian additions are not so utterly discordant as one would expect! Hernan Ruiz did the work well, even though it was work he might conveniently have been drawn and quartered for doing. Typically Spanish in its fine proportion, in its exuberance of fantastic decoration, his church is a masterpiece of plateresque architecture. Nor are the priests entirely out of harmony with the building wherein they worship. For an hour they had sung Vespers, and the deep voices of the canons, chaunting monotonously, rang weird and long among the columns; but they finished, and left the choir one by one, walking silently across the church to the sacristy. The black cassock and the scarlet hood made a fine contrast, while the short cambric surplice added to the costume a most delicate grace. One of them paused to speak with two ladies in mantillas, and the three made a picturesque group, suggesting all manner of old Spanish romance.

VII

The Court of Oranges

I went into the cathedral from the side and issuing by another door, found myself in the Court of Oranges. The setting sun touched it with warm light and overhead the sky was wonderfully blue. In Moorish times the mosque was separated from the court by no dividing-wall, so that the arrangement of pillars within was continued by the even lines of orange-trees; these are of great age and size, laden with fruit, and in their copious foliage stand with a trim self-assurance that is quite imposing.

In the centre, round a fountain into which poured water from jets at the four corners, stood a number of persons with jars of earthenware and bright copper cans. One girl held herself with the fine erectness of a Caryatid, while her jar, propped against the side, filled itself with the cold, sparkling water. A youth, some vessel in his hand, leaned over in an attitude of easy grace; and looking into her eyes, appeared to pay compliments, which she heard with superb indifference. A little boy ran up, and the girl held aside her jar while he put his mouth to the spout and drank. Then, as it overflowed, she lifted it with comely motion to her head and slowly walked away.

By now the canons had unrobed, and several strolled about the court in the sun, smoking cigarettes. The acolytes with the removal of their scarlet cassocks, were become somewhat ragged urchins playing pitch and toss with much gesture and vociferation. Two of them quarrelled fiercely because one player would not yield the halfpenny he had certainly lost, and the altercation must have ended in blows if a corpulent, elderly cleric had not indignantly reproved them, and boxed their ears. A row of tattered beggars, very well contented in the sunshine, were seated on a step, likewise smoking cigarettes, and obviously they did not consider their walk of life unduly hard.

And the thought impressed itself upon me while I lingered in that peaceful spot, that there was far more to be said for the simple

19

pleasures of sense than northern folk would have us believe. The English have still much of that ancient puritanism which finds a vague sinfulness in the uncostly delights of sunshine, and colour, and ease of mind. It is well occasionally to leave the eager turmoil of great cities for such a place as this, where one may learn that there are other, more natural ways of living, that it is possible still to spend long days, undisturbed by restless passion, without regret or longing, content in the various show that nature offers, asking only that the sun should shine and the happy seasons run their course.

An English engineer whom I had seen at the hotel, approaching me, expressed the idea in his own graphic manner. 'Down here there are a good sight more beer and skittles in life than up in Sheffield!'

One canon especially interested me, a little thin man, bent and wrinkled, apparently of fabulous age, but still something of a dandy, for he wore his clothes with a certain air, as though half a century before, byronically, he had been quite a devil with the ladies. The silver buckle on his shoes was most elegant, and he protruded his foot as though the violet silk of his stocking gave him a discreet pleasure. To the very backbone he was an optimist, finding existence evidently so delightful that it did not even need rose-coloured spectacles. He was an amiable old man, perhaps a little narrow, but very indulgent to the follies of others. He had committed no sin himself—for many years: a suspicion of personal vanity is in itself proof of a pure and gentle mind; and as for the sins of others—they were probably not heinous, and at all events would gain forgiveness. The important thing, surely, was to be sound in dogma. The day wore on and the sun now shone only in a narrow space; and this the canon perambulated, smoking the end of a cigarette, the delectable frivolity of which contrasted pleasantly with his great age. He nodded affably to other priests as they passed, a pair of young men, and one obese old creature with white hair and an expression of comfortable self-esteem. He removed his hat with a great and courteous sweep when a lady of his acquaintance crossed his path. The priests basking in the warmth were like four great black cats. It was indeed a pleasant spot, and contentment oozed into one by every pore. The canon rolled himself another cigarette, smiling as he inhaled the first sweet whiffs; and one could not but think the sovereign herb must greatly ease the journey along the steep and narrow way which leads to Paradise. The smoke rose into the air lazily, and the old cleric paused now and again to look at it, the little smile of self-satisfaction breaking on his lips.

20

Up in the North, under the cold grey sky, God Almighty may be a hard taskmaster, and the Kingdom of Heaven is attained only by much endeavour; but in Cordova these things come more easily. The aged priest walks in the sun and smokes his cigarillo. Heaven is not such an inaccessible place after all. Evidently he feels that he has done his duty—with the help of Havana tobacco—in that state of life wherein it has pleased a merciful providence to place him; and St. Peter would never be so churlish as to close the golden gates in the face of an ancient canon who sauntered to them jauntily, with the fag end of a cigarette in the corner of his mouth. Let us cultivate our cabbages in the best of all possible worlds; and afterwards— Dieu pardonnera; c'est son métier.

Three months later in the Porvenir, under the heading, 'Suicide of a Priest,' I read that one of these very canons of the Cathedral at Cordova had shot himself. A report was heard, said the journal, and the Civil Guard arriving, found the man prostrate with blood pouring from his ear, a revolver by his side. He was transported to the hospital, the sacrament administered, and he died. In his pockets they found a letter, a pawn-ticket, a woman's bracelet, and some peppermint lozenges. He was thirty-five years old. The newspaper moralised as follows: 'When even the illustrious order to which the defunct belonged is tainted with such a crime, it is well to ask whither tends the incredulity of society which finds an end to its sufferings in the barrel of a revolver. Let moralists and philosophers combat with all their might this dreadful tendency; let them make even the despairing comprehend that death is not the highest good but the passage to an unknown world where, according to Christian belief, the ill deeds of this existence are punished and the virtuous rewarded.'

VIII

Cordova

Ronda, owing its peculiarities to the surrounding mountains, was not really very characteristic of the country, and might equally well have been an highland townlet in any part of Southern Europe. But Cordova offers immediately the full sensation of Andalusia. It is absolutely a Moorish city, white and taciturn, so that you are astonished to meet people in European dress rather than Arabs, in shuffling yellow slippers. The streets are curiously silent; for the carriage, as in Tangiers, is done by mules and donkeys, which walk so quietly that you never hear them. Sometimes you are warned by a deep-voiced 'Cuidado,' but more often a pannier brushing you against the wall brings the first knowledge of their presence. On looking up you are again surprised to see not a great shining negro in a burnouse, but a Spaniard in tight trousers, with a broad-brimmed hat.

And Cordova has that sweet, exhilarating perfume of Andalusia than which nothing gives more vividly the complete feeling of the country. Those travellers must be obtuse of nostril who do not recognise different smells, grateful or offensive, in different places; no other peculiarity is more distinctive, so that an odour crossing by chance one's sense is able to recall suddenly all the complicated impressions of a strange land. When I return from England it is always that subtle fragrance which first strikes me, a mingling in warm sunlight of orange-blossom, incense, and cigarette smoke; and two whiffs of a certain brand of tobacco are sufficient to bring back to me Seville, the most enchanting of all my memories. I suppose that nowhere else are cigarettes consumed so incessantly; for in Andalusia it is not only certain classes who use them, but every one, without distinction of age or station—from the ragamuffin selling lottery-tickets in the street to the portly, solemn priest, to the burly countryman, the shop-keeper, the soldier. After all, no better means of killing time have ever been devised, and consequently to smoke them affords an occupation which most thoroughly suits the Spaniard.

I looked at Cordova from the bell-tower of the cathedral. The roofs, very lovely in their diversity of colour, were of rounded tiles, fading with every variety of delicate shade from russet and brown to yellow and the tenderest green. From the courtyards, here and there, rose a tall palm, or an orange-tree, like a dash of jade against the brilliant sun. The houses, plainly whitewashed, have from the outside so mean a look that it is surprising to find them handsome and spacious within. They are built, Moorish fashion, round a patio, which in Cordova at least is always gay with flowers. When you pass the iron gates and note the contrast between the snowy gleaming of the street and that southern greenery, the suggestion is inevitable of charming people who must rest there in the burning heat of summer. With those surroundings and in such a country passion grows surely like a poisonous plant. At night, in the starry darkness, how irresistible must be the flashing eyes of love, how eloquent the pleading of whispered sighs! But woe to the maid who admits the ardent lover among the orange-trees, her head reeling with the sweet intoxication of the blossom; for the Spanish gallant is fickle, quick to forget the vows he spoke so earnestly: he soon grows tired of kissing, and mounting his horse, rides fast away.

The uniformity of lime-washed houses makes Cordova the most difficult place in the world wherein to find your way. The streets are exactly alike, so narrow that a carriage could hardly pass, paved with rough cobbles, and tortuous: their intricacy is amazing, labyrinthine; they wind in and out of one another, leading nowhither; they meander on for half a mile and stop suddenly, or turn back, so that you are forced to go in the direction you came. You may wander for hours, trying to find some point that from the steeple appeared quite close. Sometimes you think they are interminable.

IX

The Bridge of Calahorra

The bridge that the Moors built over the Guadalquivir straggles across the water with easy arches. Somewhat dilapidated and very beautiful, it has not the strenuous look of such things in England, and the mere sight of it fills you with comfort. The clustered houses, with an added softness from the light burning mellow on their roofs and on their white walls, increase the happy impression that the world is not necessarily hurried and toilful. And the town, separated from the river by no formal embankment, lounges at the water's edge like a giant, prone on the grass and lazy, stretching his limbs after the mid-day sleep.

There is no precipitation in such a place as Cordova; life is quite long enough for all that it is really needful to do; to him who waits come all things, and a little waiting more or less can be of no great consequence. Let everything be taken very leisurely, for there is ample time. Yet in other parts of Andalusia they say the Cordovese are the greatest liars and the biggest thieves in Spain, which points to considerable industry. The traveller, hearing this, will doubtless ask what business has the pot to call the kettle black; and it is true that the standard of veracity throughout the country is by no means high. But this can scarcely be termed a vice, for the Andalusians see in it nothing discreditable, and it can be proved as exactly as a proposition of Euclid that vice and virtue are solely matters of opinion. In Southern Spain bosom friends lie to one another with complete freedom; no man would take his wife's word, but would believe only what he thought true, and think no worse of her when he caught her fibbing. Mendacity is a thing so perfectly understood that no one is abashed by detection. In England most men equivocate and nearly all women, but they are ashamed to be discovered; they blush and stammer and hesitate, or fly into a passion; the wiser Spaniard laughs, shrugging his shoulders, and utters a dozen rapid falsehoods to make up for the first. It is always said that a good liar needs an excellent memory, but he wants more qualities than that—unblushing countenance, the readiest wit, a manner to beget confidence. In fact it is so difficult to lie systematically and well that the ardour of the Andalusians in that pursuit can be ascribed only to an innate characteristic. Their imaginations, indeed, are so exuberant that the bald fact is to them grotesque and painful. They are like writers in love with words for their own sake, who cannot make the plainest statement without a gay parade of epithet and metaphor. They embroider and decorate, they colour and enhance the trivial details of circumstance. They must see themselves perpetually in an attitude; they must never fail to be effective. They lie for art's sake, without reason or rhyme, from mere devilry, often when it can only harm them. Mendacity then becomes an intellectual exercise, such as the poet's sonneteering to an imaginary lady-love.

But the Cordovan very naturally holds himself in no such unflattering estimation. The motto of his town avers that he is a warlike person and a wise one:

> Cordoba, casa de guerrera gente
> Y de sabiduria clara fuente!

And the history thereof, with its University and its Khalifs, bears him out. Art and science flourished there when the rest of Europe was enveloped in mediæval darkness: when our Saxon ancestors lived in dirty hovels, barbaric brutes who knew only how to kill, to eat, and to propagate their species, the Moors of Cordova cultivated all the elegancies of life from verse-making to cleanliness.

I was standing on the bridge. The river flowed tortuously through the fertile plain, broad and shallow, and in it the blue sky and the white houses of the city were brightly mirrored. In the distance, like a vapour of amethyst, rose the mountains; while at my feet, in mid-stream, there were two mills which might have been untouched since Moorish days. There had been no rain for months, the water stood very low, and here and there were little islands of dry yellow sand, on which grew reeds and sedge. In such a spot might easily have wandered the half-naked fisherman of the oriental tale, bewailing in melodious verse the hardness of his lot; since to his net came no fish, seeking a broken pot or a piece of iron wherewith to buy himself a dinner. There might he find a ring half-buried in the sand, which, when he rubbed to see if it were silver, a smoke would surely rise from the water, increasing till the light of day was obscured; and half dead with fear, he would perceive at last a gigantic body towering above him, and a voice more terrible than the thunder of Allah, crying: 'What wishest thou from thy slave, O king? Know that I am of the Jin, and Suleyman, whose name be exalted, enslaved me to the ring that thou hast found.'

In Cordova recollections of the Arabian Nights haunt you till the commonest sights assume a fantastic character, and the frankly impossible becomes mere matter of fact. You wonder whether your life is real or whether you have somehow reverted to the days when Scheherazade, with her singular air of veracity, recited such enthralling stories to her lord as to save her own life and that of many other maidens. I looked along the river and saw three slender trees bending over it, reflecting in the placid water their leafless branches, and under them knelt three women washing clothes. Were they three beautiful princesses whose fathers had been killed, and they expelled from their kingdom and thus reduced to menial occupations? Who knows? Indeed, I thought it very probable, for so many royal persons have come down in the world of late; but I did not approach them, since king's daughters under these circumstances have often lost one eye, and their morals are nearly always of the worst description.

X

Puerta del Puente

I went back to the old gate which led to the bridge. Close by, in the little place, was the hut of the consumo, the local custom-house, with officials lounging at the door or sitting straddle-legged on chairs, lazily smoking. Opposite was a tobacconist's, with the gaudy red and yellow sign, Campañia arrendataria de tabacos, and a dram-shop where three hardy Spaniards from the mountains stood drinking aguardiente. Than this, by the way, there is in the world no more insidious liquor, for at first you think its taste of aniseed and peppermint very disagreeable; but perseverance, here as in other human affairs, has its reward, and presently you develop for it a liking which time increases to enthusiasm. In Spain, the land of custom and usage, everything is done in a certain way; and there is a proper manner to drink aguardiente. To sip it would show a lamentable want of decorum. A Spaniard lifts the little glass to his lips, and with a comic, abrupt motion tosses the contents into his mouth, immediately afterwards drinking water, a tumbler of which is always given with the spirit. It is really the most epicurean of intoxicants because the charm lies in the after-taste. The water is so cool and refreshing after the fieriness; it gives, without the gasconnade, the emotion Keats experienced when he peppered his mouth with cayenne for the greater enjoyment of iced claret.

But the men wiped their mouths with their hands and came out of the wine shop, mounting their horses which stood outside—shaggy, long-haired beasts with high saddles and great box-stirrups. They rode slowly through the gate one after the other, in the easy slouching way of men who have been used to the saddle all their lives and in the course of the week are accustomed to go a good many miles in an easy jog-trot to and from the town. It seems to me that the Spaniards resolve themselves into types more distinctly than is usual in northern countries, while between individuals there is less difference. These three, clean-shaven and uniformly dressed, of middle size, stout, with heavy strong features and small eyes, certainly resembled one another very strikingly. They were the typical inn-keepers of Goya's pictures but obviously could not all keep inns; doubtless they were farmers, horse-dealers, or forage-merchants, shrewd men of business, with keen eyes for the main chance. That class is the most trustworthy in Spain, kind, hospitable, and honest; they are old-fashioned people with many antique customs, and preserve much of the courteous dignity which made their fathers famous.

A string of grey donkeys came along the bridge, their panniers earth-laden, poor miserable things that plodded slowly and painfully, with heads bent down, placing one foot before the other with the donkey's peculiar motion, patiently doing a thing they had patiently done ever since they could bear a load. They seemed to have a dull feeling that it was no use to make a fuss, or to complain; it would just go on till they dropped down dead and their carcases were sold for leather and glue. There was a Spanish note in the red trappings, braided and betasselled, but all worn, discoloured and stained.

Inside the gate they stopped, waiting in a huddled group, with the same heavy patience, for the examination of the consumo. An officer of the custom-house went round with a long steel prong, which he ran into the baskets one by one, to see that there was nothing dutiable hidden in the earth. Then, sparing of his words, he made a sign to the driver and sat down again straddle-wise on his chair. 'Arre, burra!' The first donkey walked slowly on, and as they heard the tinkling of the leader's bell the rest stepped forward in the long line, their heads hanging down, with that hopeless movement of the feet.

In the night, wandering at random through the streets, their silent whiteness filled me again with that intoxicating sensation of the Arabian Nights. I looked through the iron gateways as I passed, into the patios with their dark foliage, and once I heard the melancholy twang of a guitar. I was sure that in one of those houses the three princesses had thrown off their disguise and sat radiant in queenly beauty, their raven tresses falling in a hundred plaits over their shoulders, their fingers stained with henna and their long eyelashes darkened with kohl. But alas! though I lost my way I found them not.

Yet many an amorous Spaniard, too passionate to be admitted within his mistress' house, stood at her window. This method of philandering, surely most conducive to the ideal, is variously known as comer hierro, to eat iron, and pelar la pava, to pluck the turkey. One imagines that the cold air of a winter's night must render the most ardent lover platonic. It is a significant fact that in Spanish novels if the hero is left for two minutes alone with the heroine there are invariably asterisks and some hundred pages later a baby. So it is doubtless wise to separate true love by iron bars, and perchance beauty's eyes flash more darkly to the gallant standing without the gate; illusions, the magic flower of passion, arise more willingly. But in Spain the blood of youth is very hot, love laughs at most restraints and notwithstanding these precautions, often enough there is a catastrophe. The Spaniard, who will seduce any girl he can, is pitiless under like circumstances to his own womenkind; so there is much weeping, the girl is turned out of doors and falls readily into the hands of the procuress. In the brothels of Seville or of Madrid she finds at least a roof and bread to eat; and the fickle swain goes his way rejoicing.

I found myself at last near the Puerta del Puente, and I stood again on the Moorish bridge. The town was still and mysterious in the night, and the moon shone down on the water with a hard and brilliant coldness. The three trees with their bare branches looked yet more slender, naked and alone, like pre-Raphaelite trees in a landscape of Pélléas et Mélisande; the broad river, almost stagnant, was extraordinarily calm and silent. I wondered what strange things the placid Guadalquivir had seen through the centuries; on its bosom many a body had been borne towards the sea. It recalled those mysterious waters of the Eastern tales which brought to the marble steps of palaces great chests in which lay a fair youth's headless corpse or a sleeping beautiful maid.

XI

Seville

The impression left by strange towns and cities is often a matter of circumstance, depending upon events in the immediate past; or on the chance which, during his earliest visit, there befell the traveller. After a stormy passage across the Channel, Newhaven, from the mere fact of its situation on solid earth, may gain a fascination which closer acquaintance can never entirely destroy; and even Birmingham, first seen by a lurid sunset, may so affect the imagination as to appear for ever like some infernal, splendid city, restless with the hurried toil of gnomes and goblins. So to myself Seville means ten times more than it can mean to others. I came to it after weary years in London, heartsick with much hoping, my mind dull with drudgery; and it seemed a land of freedom. There I became at last conscious of my youth, and it seemed a belvedere upon a new life. How can I forget the delight of wandering in the Sierpes, released at length from all imprisoning ties, watching the various movement as though it were a stage-play, yet half afraid that the falling curtain would bring back reality! The songs, the dances, the happy idleness of orange-gardens, the gay turbulence of Seville by night; ah! there at least I seized life eagerly, with both hands, forgetting everything but that time was short and existence full of joy. I sat in the warm sunshine, inhaling the pleasant odours, reminding myself that I had no duty to do then, or the morrow, or the day after. I lay a-bed thinking how happy, effortless and free would be my day. Mounting my horse, I clattered through the narrow streets, over the cobbles, till I came to the country; the air was fresh and sweet, and Aguador loved the spring mornings. When he put his feet to the springy turf he gave a little shake of pleasure, and without a sign from me broke into a gallop. To the amazement of shepherds guarding their wild flocks, to the confusion of herds of brown pigs, scampering hastily as we approached, he and I excited by the wind singing in our ears, we pelted madly through the country. And the whole land laughed with the joy of living.

But I love also the recollection of Seville in the grey days of

December, when the falling rain offered a grateful contrast to the unvarying sunshine. Then new sights delighted the eye, new perfumes the nostril. In the decay of that long southern autumn a more sombre opulence was added to the gay colours; a different spirit filled the air, so that I realised suddenly that old romantic Spain of Ferdinand and Isabella. It lay a-dying still, gorgeous in corruption, sober yet flamboyant, rich and poverty-stricken, squalid, magnificent. The white streets, the dripping trees, the clouds gravid with rain, gave to all things an adorable melancholy, a sad, poetic charm. Looking back, I cannot dismiss the suspicion that my passionate emotions were somewhat ridiculous, but at twenty-three one can afford to lack a sense of humour.

But Seville at first is full of disillusion. It has offered abundant material to the idealist who, as might be expected, has drawn of it a picture which is at once common and pretentious. Your idealist can see no beauty in sober fact, but must array it in all the theatrical properties of a vulgar imagination; he must give to things more imposing proportions, he colours gaudily; Nature for him is ever posturing in the full glare of footlights. Really he stands on no higher level than the housemaid who sees in every woman a duchess in black velvet, an Aubrey Plantagenet in plain John Smith. So I, in common with many another traveller, expected to find in the Guadalquivir a river of transparent green, with orange-groves along its banks, where wandered ox-eyed youths and maidens beautiful. Palm-trees, I thought, rose towards heaven, like passionate souls longing for release from earthly bondage; Spanish women, full-breasted and sinuous, danced boleros, fandangos, while the air rang with the joyous sound of castanets, and toreadors in picturesque habiliments twanged the light guitar.

Alas! the Guadalquivir is like yellow mud, and moored to the busy quays lie cargo-boats lading fruit or grain or mineral; there no perfume scents the heavy air. The nights, indeed, are calm and clear, and the stars shine brightly; but the river banks see no amours more romantic than those of stokers from Liverpool or Glasgow, and their lady-loves have neither youth nor beauty.

Yet Seville has many a real charm to counter-balance these lost illusions. He that really knows it, like an ardent lover with his mistress' imperfections, would have no difference; even the Guadalquivir, so matter-of-fact, really so prosaic, has an unimagined attractiveness; the crowded shipping, the hurrying

31

porters, add to that sensation of vivacity which is of Seville the most fascinating characteristic. And Seville is an epitome of Andalusia, with its life and death, with its colour and vivid contrasts, with its boyish gaiety.

It is a city of delightful ease, of freedom and sunshine, of torrid heat. There it does not matter what you do, nor when, nor how you do it. There is none to hinder you, none to watch. Each takes his ease, and is content that his neighbour should do the like. Doubtless people are lazy in Seville, but good heavens! why should one be so terribly strenuous? Go into the Plaza Nueva, and you will see it filled with men of all ages, of all classes, 'taking the sun'; they promenade slowly, untroubled by any mental activity, or sit on benches between the palm-trees, smoking cigarettes; perhaps the more energetic read the bull-fighting news in the paper. They are not ambitious, and they do not greatly care to make their fortunes; so long as they have enough to eat and drink—food is very cheap—and cigarettes to smoke, they are quite happy. The Corporation provides seats, and the sun shines down for nothing—so let them sit in it and warm themselves. I daresay it is as good a way of getting through life as most others.

A southern city never reveals its true charm till the summer, and few English know what Seville is under the burning sun of July. It was built for the great heat, and it is only then that the refreshing coolness of the patio can be appreciated. In the streets the white glare is mitigated by awnings that stretch from house to house, and the half light in the Sierpes, the High Street, has a curious effect; the people in their summer garb walk noiselessly, as though the warmth made sound impossible. Towards evening the sail-cloths are withdrawn, and a breath of cold air sinks down; the population bestirs itself, and along the Sierpes the cafés become suddenly crowded and noisy.

Then, for it was too hot to ride earlier, I would mount my horse and cross the river. The Guadalquivir had lost its winter russet, and under the blue sky gained varied tints of liquid gold, of emerald and of sapphire. I lingered in Triana, the gipsy-quarter, watching the people. Beautiful girls stood at the windows, so that the whole way was lined with them, and their lips were not unwilling to break into charming smiles. One especially I remember who was used to sit on a balcony at a street-corner; her hair was irreproachable in its elaborate arrangement, and the red carnation in it gleamed like fire against the night. Her face was long, fairer-complexioned than is common, with regular and delicate features. She sat at her balcony, with a huge book open on her knee, which she read with studied disregard of the passers-by; but when I looked back sometimes I saw that she had lifted her eyes, lustrous and dark, and they met mine gravely.

And in the country I passed through long fields of golden corn, which reached as far as I could see; I remembered the spring, when it had all been new, soft, fresh, green. And presently I turned round to look at Seville in the distance, bathed in brilliant light, glowing as though its walls were built of yellow flame. The Giralda arose in its wonderful grace like an arrow; so slim, so comely, it reminded one of an Arab youth, with long, thin limbs. With the setting sun, gradually the city turned rosy-red and seemed to lose all substantiality, till it became a many-shaped mist that was dissolved in the tenderness of the sky.

Late in the night I stood at my window looking at the cloudless heaven. From the earth ascended, like incense, the mellow odours of summer-time; the belfry of the neighbouring church stood boldly outlined against the darkness, and the storks that had built their nest upon it were motionless, not stirring even as the bells rang out the hours. The city slept, and it seemed that I alone watched in the silence; the sky still was blue, and the stars shone in their countless millions. I thought of the city that never rested, of London with its unceasing roar, the endless streets, the greyness. And all around me was a quiet serenity, a tranquillity such as the Christian may hope shall reward him in Paradise for the troublous pilgrimage of life. But that is long ago and passed for ever.

XII

The Alcazar

Arriving at Seville the recollection of Cordova took me quickly to the Alcazar; but I was a little disappointed. It has been ill and tawdrily restored, with crude pigments, with gold that is too bright and too clean; but even before that, Charles V. and his successors had made additions out of harmony with Moorish feeling. Of the palace where lived the Mussulman Kings nothing, indeed, remains; but Pedro the Cruel, with whom the edifice now standing is more especially connected, was no less oriental than his predecessors, and he employed Morisco architects to rebuild it. Parts are said to be exact reproductions of the older structure, while many of the beautiful tiles were taken from Moorish houses.

The atmosphere, then, is but half Arabic; the rest belongs to that flaunting, multi-coloured barbarism which is characteristic of Northern Spain before the union of Arragon and Castile. Wandering in the deserted courts, looking through horseshoe windows of exquisite design at the wild garden, Pedro the Cruel and Maria de Padilla are the figures that occupy the mind.

Seville teems with anecdotes of the monarch who, according to the point of view, has been called the Cruel and the Just. He was an amorist for whom platonic dalliance had no charm, and there are gruesome tales of ladies burned alive because they would not quench the flame of his desires, of others, fiercely virtuous, who poured boiling oil on face and bosom to make themselves unattractive in his sight. But the head that wears a crown apparently has fascinations which few women can resist, and legend tells more frequently of Pedro's conquests than of his rebuffs. He was an ardent lover to whom marriage vows were of no importance; that he committed bigamy is certain—and pardonable, but some historians are inclined to think that he had at one and the same time no less than three wives. He was oriental in his tastes.

In imitation of the Paynim sovereigns Pedro loved to wander in the streets of Seville at night, alone and disguised, to seek adventure or to see for himself the humour of his subjects; and like them also it pleased him to administer justice seated in the porch of his palace. If he was often hard and proud towards the nobles, with the people he was always very gracious; to them he was the redressor of wrongs and a protector of the oppressed; his justice was that of the Mussulman rulers, rapid, terrible and passionate, often quaint. For instance: a rich priest had done some injury to a cobbler, who brought him before the ecclesiastical tribunals, where he was for a year suspended from his clerical functions. The tradesman thought the punishment inadequate, and taking the law into his own hands gave the priest a drubbing. He was promptly seized, tried, condemned to death. But he appealed to the king who, with a witty parody of the rival Court, changed the punishment to suspension from his trade, and ordered the cobbler for twelve months to make no boots.

On the other hand, the Alcazar itself has been the scene of Pedro's vilest crimes, in the whole list of which is none more insolent, none more treacherous, than that whereby he secured the priceless ruby which graces still the royal crown of England. There is a school of historians which insists on finding a Baptist Minister in every hero—think what a poor-blooded creature they wish to make of the glorious Nelson—but no casuistry avails to cleanse the memory of Pedro of Castille: even for his own ruthless age he was a monster of cruelty and lust. Indeed the indignation with which his biographers have felt bound to charge their pens has somewhat obscured their judgment; they have so eagerly insisted on the censure with which themselves regard their hero's villainies, that they have found little opportunity to explain a complex character. Yet the story of his early life affords a simple key to his maturity. Till the age of fifteen he lived in prisons, suffering with his mother every insult and humiliation, while his father's mistress kept queenly state, and her children received the honours of royal princes. When he came to the throne he found himself a catspaw between his natural brothers and ambitious nobles. His nearest relatives were ever his bitterest enemies, and he was continually betrayed by those he trusted; even his mother delivered to the rebellious peers the strongholds and the treasures he had left in her charge and caused him to be taken prisoner. As a boy he had been violent and impetuous, yet always loyal: but before he was twenty he became suspicious and mistrustful; in his weakness he made craft and perfidy his weapons, practising to compose his face, to feign forgetfulness of injury till the moment of vengeance; he learned to dissemble so that none could tell his mind, and treated no courtiers with greater favour than those upon whose death he had already determined.

Intermingled with this career of vice and perfidy and bloodshed is the love of Maria de Padilla, whom the king met when he was eighteen, and till her death loved passionately—with brief inconstancies, for fidelity has never been a royal virtue; and she figures with gentle pathos in that grim history like wild perfumed flowers on a storm-beaten coast. After the assassination of the unfortunate Blanche, the French Queen whom he loathed with an extraordinary physical repulsion, Pedro acknowledged a secret marriage with Maria de Padilla, which legitimised her children; but for ten years before she had been treated with royal rights. The historian says that she was very beautiful, but her especial charm seems to have been that voluptuous grace which is characteristic of Andalusian women. She was simple and pious, with a nature of great sweetness, and she never abused her power; her influence, as runs the hackneyed phrase, was always for good, and untiringly she did her utmost to incline her despot lover to mercy. She alone sheds a ray of light on Pedro's memory, only her love can save him from the execration of posterity. When she died rich and poor alike mourned her, and the king was inconsolable. He honoured her with pompous obsequies, and throughout the kingdom ordered masses to be sung for the rest of her soul.

The guardians of the Alcazar show you the chambers in which dwelt this gracious lady, and the garden-fountain wherein she bathed in summer. Moralists, anxious to prove that the way of righteousness is hard, say that beauty dies, but they err, for beauty is immortal. The habitations of a lovely woman never lose the enchantment she has cast over them, her comeliness lingers in their empty chambers like a subtle odour; and centuries after her very bones have crumbled to dust it is her presence alone that is felt, her footfall that is heard on the marble floors.

Garish colours, alas! have driven the tender spirit of Maria de Padilla from the royal palace, but it has betaken itself to the old garden, and there wanders sadly. It is a charming place of rare plants and exotic odours; cypress and tall palm trees rise towards the blue sky with their irresistible melancholy, their far-away suggestion of burning deserts; and at their feet the ground is carpeted with violets. Yet to me the wild roses brought strangely recollections of England, of long summer days when the air was sweet and balmy; the birds sang heavenly songs, the same songs as they sing in June in the fat Kentish fields. The gorgeous palace had only suggested the long past days of history, and Seville the joy of life and the love of sunshine; but the old quiet garden took me far away from Spain, so that I longed to be again in England. In thought I wandered through a garden that I knew in years gone by, filled also with flowers, but with hollyhocks and jasmine; the breeze carried the sweet scent of the honeysuckle to my nostrils, and I looked at the green lawns, with the broad, straight lines of the grass-mower. The low of cattle reached my ears, and wandering to the fence I looked into the fields beyond; yellow cows grazed idly or lay still chewing the cud; they stared at me with listless, sleepy eyes.

But I glanced up and saw a flock of wild geese flying northwards in long lines that met, making two sides of a huge triangle; they flew quickly in the cloudless sky, far above me, and presently were lost to view. About me was the tall box-wood of the southern garden, and tropical plants with rich flowers of yellow and red and purple. A dark fir-tree stood out, ragged and uneven, like a spirit of the North, erect as a life without reproach; but the foliage of the palms hung down with a sad, adorable grace.

XIII

Calle de las Sierpes

In Seville the Andalusian character thrives in its finest flower; and
nowhere can it be more conveniently studied than in the narrow,
sinuous, crowded thoroughfare which is the oddest street in Europe.
The Calle de las Sierpes is merely a pavement, hardly broader than
that of Piccadilly, without a carriage-way. The houses on either side
are very irregular; some are tall, four-storeyed, others quite tiny;
some are well kept and freshly painted, others dilapidated. It is one
of the curiosities of Seville that there is no particularly fashionable
quarter; and, as though some moralising ruler had wished to place
before his people a continual reminder of the uncertainty of human
greatness, by the side of a magnificent palace you will find a hovel.

At no hour of the day does the Calle de las Sierpes lack animation,
but to see it at its best you must go towards evening, at seven
o'clock, for then there is scarcely room to move. Fine gentlemen
stand at the club doors or sit within, looking out of the huge
windows; the merchants and the students, smoking cigarettes,
saunter, wrapped magnificently in their capos. Cigarette-girls pass
with roving eyes; they suffer from no false modesty and smile with
pleasure when a compliment reaches their ears. Admirers do not
speak in too low a tone and the fair Sevillan is never hard of hearing.

Newspaper boys with shrill cries announce evening editions:
'Porvenir! Noticiero!' Vendors of lottery-tickets wander up and
down, audaciously offering the first prize: 'Quien quiere el premio
gardo?' Beggars follow you with piteous tales of fasts improbably
extended. But most striking is the gente flamenca, the bull-fighter,
with his numerous hangers-on. The toreros—toreador is an
unknown word, good for comic opera and persons who write novels
of Spanish life and cannot be bothered to go to Spain—the toreros
sit in their especial cafe, the Cerveceria National, or stand in little
groups talking to one another. They are distinguishable by the
coleta, which is a little plait of hair used to attach the chignon of
full-dress: it is the dearest ambition of the aspirant to the bull-ring
to possess this ornament; he grows it as soon as he is full-fledged,

38

and it is solemnly cut off when the weight of years and the responsibility of landed estates induce him to retire from the profession. The bull-fighter dresses peculiarly and the gente flamenca, imitates him so far as its means allow. A famous matador is as well paid as in England a Cabinet Minister or a music-hall artiste. This is his costume: a broad-brimmed hat with a low crown, which is something like a topper absurdly flattened down, with brims preposterously broadened out. The front of his shirt is befrilled and embroidered, and his studs are the largest diamonds; not even financiers in England wear such important stones. He wears a low collar without a necktie, but ties a silk handkerchief round his neck like an English navvy; an Eton jacket, fitting very tightly, brown, black, or grey, with elaborate frogs and much braiding; the trousers, skin-tight above, loosen below, and show off the lower extremities when, like the heroes of feminine romance, the wearer has a fine leg. Indeed, it is a mode of dress which exhibits the figure to great advantage, and many of these young men have admirable forms.

In their strong, picturesque way they are often very handsome. They have a careless grace of gesture, a manner of actors perfectly at ease in an effective part, a brutal healthiness; there is a flamboyance in their bearing, a melodramatic swagger, which is most diverting. And their faces, so contrasted are the colours, so strongly marked the features, are full of interest. Clean shaven, the beard shows violet through the olive skin; they have high cheek bones and thin, almost hollow cheeks, with eyes set far back in the sockets, dark and lustrous under heavy brows. The black hair, admirably attached to the head, is cut short; shaved on the temples and over the ears, brushed forward as in other countries is fashionable with gentlemen of the box: it fits the skull like a second, tighter skin. The lips are red and sensual, the teeth white, regular and well shaped. The bull-fighter is remarkable also for the diamond rings which decorate his fingers and the massive gold, the ponderous seals, of his watch-chain.

Who can wonder then that maidens fair, their hearts turning to thoughts of love, should cast favourable glances upon this hero of a hundred fights? The conquests of tenors and grand-dukes and fiddlers are insignificant beside those of a bull-fighter; and the certainty of feminine smiles is another inducement for youth to exchange the drudgery of menial occupations for the varied excitement of the ring.

At night the Sierpes is different again. Little by little the people scatter to their various homes, the shops are closed, the clubs put out their lights, and by one the loiterers are few. The contrast is vivid between the noisy throng of day-time and this sudden stillness; the emptiness of the winding street seems almost unnatural. The houses, losing all variety, are intensely black; and above, the sinuous line of sky is brilliant with clustering stars. A drunken roysterer reels from a tavern-door, his footfall echoing noisily along the pavement, but quickly he sways round a corner; and the silence, more impressive for the interruption, returns. The night-watchman, huddled in a cloak of many folds, is sleeping in a doorway, dimly outlined by the yellow gleam of his lantern.

Then I, a lover of late hours, returning, seek the guardia. Sevillan houses are locked at midnight by this individual, who keeps the latch-keys of a whole street, and is supposed to be on the look-out for tardy comers. I clap my hands, such being the Spanish way to attract attention, and shout; but he does not appear. He is a good-natured, round man, bibulous, with grey hair and a benevolent manner. I know his habits and resign myself to inquiring for him in the neighbouring dram-shops. I find him at last and assail him with all the abuse at my command; he is too tipsy to answer or to care, and follows me, jangling his keys. He fumbles with them at the door, blaspheming because they are so much alike, and finally lets me in.

'Buena noche. Descanse v bien.'

XIV

Characteristics

It is a hazardous thing to attempt the analysis of national character, for after all, however careful the traveller may be in his inquiries, it is from the few individuals himself has known that his most definite impressions are drawn. Of course he can control his observations by asking the opinion of foreigners long resident in the country; but curiously enough in Andalusia precisely the opposite occurs from what elsewhere is usual. Aliens in England, France, or Italy, with increasing comprehension, acquire also affection and esteem for the people among whom they live; but I have seldom found in Southern Spain a foreigner—and there are many, merchants, engineers and the like, with intimate knowledge of the inhabitants—who had a good word to say for the Andalusians.

But perhaps it is in the behaviour of crowds that the most accurate picture of national character can be obtained. Like composite photographs which give the appearance of a dozen people together, but a recognisable portrait of none, the multitude offers as it were a likeness in the rough, without precision of detail yet with certain marked features more obviously indicated. The crowd is an individual without responsibility, unoppressed by the usual ties of prudence and decorum, who betrays himself because he lacks entirely self-consciousness and the desire to pose. In Spain the crowd is above all things good-humoured, fond of a joke so long as it is none too subtle, excitable of course and prone to rodomontade, yet practical, eager to make the best of things and especially to get its money's worth. If below the surface there are a somewhat brutal savagery, a cruel fickleness, these are traits common with all human beings together assembled; they are merely evidence of man's close relationship to ape and tiger.

From contemporary novels more or less the same picture appears, and also from the newspapers, though in these somewhat idealised; for the Press, bound to flatter for its living, represents its patrons, as do some portrait-painters, not as they are but as they would like to be. In the eyes of Andalusian journalists their compatriots are for

41

ever making a magnificent gesture; and the condition would be absurd if a hornet's nest of comic papers, tempering vanity with a lively sense of the ridiculous, did not save the situation by abundantly coarse caricatures.

It is vanity then which emerges as the most distinct of national traits, a vanity so egregious, so childish, so grotesque, that the onlooker is astounded. The Andalusians have a passion for gorgeous raiment and for jewellery. They must see themselves continually in the brightest light, standing for ever on some alpine eminence of vice or virtue, in full view of their fellow men. Like schoolboys they will make themselves out desperate sinners to arouse your horror, and if that does not impress you, accomplished actors ready to suit your every mood, they will pose as saints than whom none more truly pious have existed on the earth. They are the Gascons of Spain, but beside them the Bordelais is a truthful, unimaginative creature.

Next comes laziness. There is in Europe no richer soil than that of Andalusia, and the Arabs, with an elaborate system of irrigation, obtained three crops a year; but now half the land lies uncultivated, and immense tracts are planted only with olives, which, comparatively, entail small labour. But the inhabitants of this fruitful country are happy in this, that boredom is unknown to them; content to lie in the sun for hours, neither talking, thinking, nor reading, they are never tired of idleness: two men will sit for half a day in a cafe, with a glass of water before them, not exchanging three remarks in an hour. I fancy it is this stolidness which has given travellers an impression of dignity; in their quieter moments they remind one of very placid sheep, for they have not half the energy of pigs, which in Spain at least are restless and spirited creatures. But a trifle will rouse them; and then, quite unable to restrain themselves, pallid with rage, they hurl abuse at their enemy—Spanish, they say, is richer in invective than any other European tongue—and quickly long knives are whipped out to avenge the affront.

Universal opinion has given its verdict in an epithet: and just as many people speak of the volatile Frenchman, the stolid Dutchman, the amatory Italian, they talk of the proud Spaniard. But it is pride of a peculiar sort; a Sevillian with only the smallest claims to respectability would rather die than carry a parcel through the street; however poor, some one must perform for him so menial an office: and he would consider it vastly beneath his dignity to accept charity, though if he had the chance would not hesitate to swindle you out of sixpence. But in matters of honesty these good people show a certain discrimination. Your servants, for example, would hesitate to steal money, especially if liable to detection, but not to take wine and sugar and oil: which is proved by the freedom with which they discuss the theft among themselves and the calmness with which they acknowledge it when a wrathful master takes them in the act. The reasoning is, if you're such a fool as not to keep your things under lock and key you deserve to be robbed; and if dismissed for such a peccadillo they consider themselves very hardly used.

Uncharitable persons, saying that a Spaniard will live for a week on bread and water duly to prepare himself for a meal at another's expense, accuse them of gluttony; but I have always found the Andalusians abstemious eaters, nor have I wondered at this, since Spanish food is abominable. But drunkards they often are. I should think as many people in proportion get drunk in Seville as in London, though it is only fair to add that their heads are not strong, and very little alcohol will produce in them an indecent exhilaration.

But if the reader, because the Andalusians are slothful, truthless, but moderately honest, vain, concludes that they are an unattractive people he will grossly err. His reasoning, that moral qualities make pleasant companions, is quite false; on the contrary it is rigid principles and unbending character, strength of will and a decided sense of right and wrong, which make intercourse difficult. A sensitive conscience is no addition to the amenities of the dinner-table. But when a man is willing to counter a deadly sin with a shrug of the shoulders, when between white and black he can discover no insupportable contrast, the probabilities are that he will at least humour your whims and respect your prejudices. And so it is that the Andalusians make very agreeable acquaintance. They are free and amiable in their conversation, and will always say the thing that pleases rather than the brutal thing that is. They miss no opportunity to make compliments, which they do so well that at the moment you are assured these flattering remarks come from the bottom of their hearts. Very reasonably, they cannot understand why you should be disagreeable to a man merely because you rob him; to injury, unless their minds are clouded by passion, they have not the bad taste to add insult. Compare with these manners the British abhorrence of polite and complimentary speeches, especially if they happen to be true: the Englishman may hold you in the highest estimation, but wild horses will not drag from him an acknowledgment of the fact; whereby humanism and the general stock of self-esteem are notably diminished.

Nothing can be more graceful than their mode of speech, for the very construction of the language conduces to courtesy. The Spaniards have also an oriental way of offering you things, placing themselves and their houses entirely at your disposal. If you remark on anything of theirs they beg you at once to take it. If you go into a pot-house where a peasant is dining on a plate of ham, a few olives, and a glass of wine, he will ask: 'Le gusta,' 'Will you have some,' with a little motion of handing you his meal. Of course it would be an outrage to decorum to accept these generous offers, but that is beside the question; for good manners are not an affair of the heart, but a complicated game to be learned and played on either side with due attention to the rules. It may be argued that such details are not serious; but surely for the common round of life politeness is more necessary than any heroic qualities. We need our friends' self-sacrifice once in a blue moon, but their courtesy every day; and for my own part, I would choose the companions of my leisure rather for their good breeding than for the excellence of their dispositions.

Beside this, however, the Andalusians are much attached to children, and it is pleasant to see the real fondness which exists between various members of a family. One singular point I have noted, that although the Spanish marry for love rather than from convenience, a wife puts kindred before husband, her affection remaining chiefly where it was before marriage. But if the moralist desires yet more solid virtues, he need only inquire of the first Sevillan he meets, who will give at shortest notice, in choice and fluent language, a far more impressive list than I could ever produce.

XV

Don Juan Tenorio

On its own behalf each country seems to choose one man, historical or imaginary, to stand for the race, making as it were an incarnation of all the virtues and all the vices wherewith it is pleased to charge itself; and nothing really better explains the character of a people than their choice of a national hero. Fifty years ago John Bull was the typical Englishman. Stout, rubicund and healthy, with a loud voice and a somewhat aggressive manner, he belonged distinctly to the middle classes. He had a precise idea of his rights and a flattering opinion of his merits; he was peaceable, but ready enough to fight for commercial advantages, or if roused, for conscience sake. And when this took place he possessed always the comforting assurance that the Almighty was on his side; he put his faith without hesitation on the Bible and on the superiority of the English Nation. For foreigners he had a magnificent contempt and distinguished between them and monkeys only by a certain mental effort. Art he thought nasty, literature womanish; he was a Tory, middle-aged and well-to-do.

But nowadays all that is changed; John Bull, having amassed great wealth, has been gathered to his fathers and now disports himself in an early Victorian paradise furnished with horse-hair sofas and mahogany sideboards. His son reigns in his stead; and though perhaps not officially recognised as England's archetype, his appearance in novel and in drama, in the illustrated papers, in countless advertisements, proves the reality of his sway. It is his image that rests in the heart of British maidens, his the example that British youths industriously follow.

But John Bull, Junior, has added his mother's maiden name to his own, and remembers with pleasure that he belongs to a good old county family. He has changed his address from Bedford Square to South Kensington, and has been educated at a Public School and at a University. Young, tall and fair-haired, there is nothing to suggest that he will ever have that inelegant paunch which prevented the father, even in his loftiest moments of moral indignation, from being dignified. Of course he is a soldier, for the army is still the only profession for a gentleman, and England's hero is that above all things. His morals are unexceptional, since to the ten commandments of Moses he has added the decalogue of good form. His clothes, whether he wears a Norfolk jacket or a frock coat, fit to perfection. He is a good shot, a daring rider, a serviceable cricketer. His heart beats with simple emotions, he will ever cheer at the sight of the Union Jack, and the strains of Rule Britannia bring patriotic tears to his eyes. Of late, (like myself,) he has become an Imperialist. His intentions are always strictly honourable, and he would not kiss the tip of a woman's fingers except Hymen gave him the strictest rights to do so. If he became enamoured of a lady with whom such tender sentiments should not be harboured, he would invariably remember his duty at the psychological moment, and with many moving expressions renounce her: in fact he is a devil at renouncing women. I wonder it flatters them.

Contrast with this pattern of excellence, eminently praiseworthy if somewhat dull, Don Juan Tenorio, who stands in exactly the same relation to the Andalusians as does John Bull to the English. He is a worthless, heartless creature, given over to the pursuit of emotion. The main lines of the story are well known. The legend, so far as Seville is concerned, (industrious persons have found analogues throughout the world,) appears to be founded on fact. There actually lived a Comendador de Calatrava who was killed by Don Juan after the abduction of his daughter. The perfect amorist, according to the Cronica de Sevilla, was then inveigled into the church where lay his enemy and assassinated by the Franciscans, who spread the pious fiction that the image of his victim, descending from its pedestal, had itself exacted vengeance. It was an unfortunate invention, for the catastrophe has proved a stumbling-block to all that have dealt with the subject. The Spaniards of Molina's day may not have minded the clumsy deus ex machina, but later writers have been able to make nothing of it. In Molière's play, for instance, the grotesque statue is absurdly inapposite, for his Don Juan is a wit and a cynic, a courtier of Louis XIV., with whose sins avenging gods are out of all proportion. Love for him is an intellectual exercise and a pastime. 'Constancy,' he says, 'is only good for fools. We owe ourselves to pretty women in general, and the mere fact of having met one does not absolve us from our duty to others. The birth of passion has an inexplicable charm, and the pleasure of love is in variety.' And Zorilla, whose version is the most poetic of them all, has succeeded in giving only a ridiculous exhibition of waxworks.

But the monk, Tirso de Molina, who was the first to apply literary form to the legend, alone gives the character in its primitive simplicity. He drew the men of his time; and his compatriots, recognising themselves, have made the work immortal. For Spain, at all events, the type has been irrevocably fixed. Don Juan Tenorio was indeed a Spaniard of his age, a man of turbulent instincts, with a love of adventure and a fine contempt for danger, of an overwhelming pride; careful of his own honour, and careless of that of others. He looked upon every woman as lawful prey and hesitated at neither perjury nor violence to gain his ends; despair and tears left him indifferent. Love for him was purely carnal, with nothing of the timid flame of pastoral romance, nor of the chivalrous and metaphysic passion of Provence; it was a fierce, consuming fire which quickly burnt itself out. He was a vulgar and unoriginal seducer who stole favours in the dark by pretending to be the lady's chosen lover, or induced guileless maids to trust him under promise of marriage, then rode away as fast as his horse could carry him. The monotony of his methods and their success are an outrage to the intelligence of the sex. But for all his scoffing he remained a true Catholic, devoutly believing that the day would come when he must account for his acts; and he proposed, when too old to commit more sins, to repent and make his peace with the Almighty.

It is significant that the Andalusians have thus chosen Don Juan Tenorio, for he is an abstract, with the lines somewhat subdued by the advance of civilisation, of the national character. For them his vices, his treachery, his heartlessness, have nothing repellent; nor does his inconstancy rob him of feminine sympathy. He is, indeed, a far greater favourite with the ladies than John Bull. The Englishman they respect, they know he will make a good husband and a model father; but he is too monogamous to arouse enthusiasm.

XVI

Women of Andalusia

It is meet and just that the traveller who desires a closer acquaintance with the country wherein he sojourns than is obtained by the Cockney tripper, should fall in love. The advantages of this proceeding are manifold and obvious. He will acquire the language with a more rapid facility; he will look upon the land with greater sympathy and hence with sharper insight; and little particularities of life will become known to him, which to the dreary creature who surveys a strange world from the portico of an expensive hotel, must necessarily lie hid. If I personally did not arrive at that delectable condition the fault is with the immortal gods rather than with myself; for in my eagerness to learn the gorgeous tongue of Calderon and of Cervantes, I placed myself purposely in circumstances where I thought the darts of young Cupid could never fail to miss me. But finally I was reduced to Ollendorf's Grammar. However, these are biographical details of interest to none but myself; they are merely to serve as preface for certain observations upon the women whom the traveller in the evening sees hurrying through the Sierpes on their way home.

Human beauty is the most arbitrary of things, and the Englishman, accustomed to the classic type of his own countrywomen, will at first perhaps be somewhat disappointed with the excellence of Spain. It consists but seldom in any regularity of feature, for their appeal is to the amorist rather than to the sculptor in marble. Their red lips carry suggestions of burning kisses, so that his heart must be hard indeed who does not feel some flutterings at their aspect. The teeth are small, very white, regular. Face and body, indeed, are but the expression of a passionate nature.

But when I write of Spanish women I think of you, Rosarito; I find suddenly that it is no impersonal creature that fills my mind, but you—you! When I state solemnly that their greatest beauty lies in their hair and eyes, it is of you I think; it is your dark eyes that were lustrous, soft as velvet, caressing sometimes, and sometimes sparkling with fiery glances. (Alas! that I can find but hackneyed phrases to describe those heart-disturbers!) And when I say that the eyebrows of a Spanish woman are not often so delicately pencilled as with many an English girl, I remember that yours were thick; and the luxuriance gave you a certain tropical and savage charm. And your hair was plentiful and curling, intensely black; I believe it was your greatest care in life. Don't you remember how often you explained to me that nothing was so harmful as to brush it, and how proud you were that it hung in glorious locks to your very knees?

Hardly any girl in Seville is too poor to have a peinadora to do her hair; and these women go from house to house, combing and arranging the coiffure for such infinitesimal sums as half a real, which is little more than a penny.

Again I try to be impersonal. The complexion ranges through every quality from dark olive to pearly white; but yours, Rosarito, was like the very finest ivory, a perfect miracle of delicacy and brilliance; and the blood in the cheeks shone through with a rich, soft red. I used to think it was a colour by itself, not to be found on palettes, the carnation of your cheeks, Rosarito. And none could walk with such graceful dignity as you; it was a pleasure to watch your perfect ease, your self-command. Your feet, I think, were somewhat long; but your hands were wonderful, very small, admirably modelled, with little tapering fingers, and the most adorable filbert nails. Don't you remember how I used to look at them, and turn them over and discuss them point by point? And if ever I kissed their soft, warm palms, (I think it possible, though I have no vivid recollections,) remember that I was twenty-three; and it was certainly an appropriate gesture in the little comedy which to our mutual entertainment we played so gravely.

Now, as I write, my heart goes pit-a-pat, thinking of you, Rosarito; and I'm sure that if we had over again that charming time, I should fall head over ears in love. Oh, you know we were both fibbing when we vowed we adored one another; I am a romancer by profession, and you by nature. We parted joyously, and you had the grace not to force a tear, and neither of our hearts was broken. Where are you now, I wonder; and do you ever think of me?

The whole chapter of Andalusian beauty is unfolded in the tobacco factory at Seville. Six thousand women work there, at little tables placed by the columns which uphold the roof; they are of all ages, of all types; plain, pretty, commonplace, beautiful; and ten, perhaps, are lovely. The gipsies are disappointing, not so comely as the pure Spaniards; and they attract only by the sphinx-like mystery of their copper-coloured skin, by their hard, unfathomable eyes.

The Sevillans are perhaps inclined to stoutness, but that is a charm in their lover's sight, and often have a little down on the upper lip, than which, when it amounts to no more than a shadow, nothing can be more enchanting. They look with malicious eyes as you saunter through room after room in the factory; it is quite an experience to run the gauntlet of their numerous tongues, making uncomplimentary remarks about your person, sometimes to your embarrassment offering you the carnation from their hair, or other things. Their clothes are suspended to the pillars, and their costume in summer is more adapted for coolness than for the inspection of decorous foreigners. They may bring with them babies, and many a girl will have a cradle by her side, which she rocks with one foot as her fingers work nimbly at the cigarettes.

They are very oriental, these women with voluptuous forms; they have no education, and with all their charm are unutterably stupid; they do not read, and find even newspapers tiresome! Those whose circumstances do not force them to work for their living, love nothing better than to lie for long hours on a sofa, neither talking nor thinking, in easy gowns, untrammelled by tight-fitting things. In the morning they put on a mantilla and go to mass, and besides, except to pay a polite visit on a friend or to drive in the Paseo, hardly leave the house. They are content with the simplest life. They adore their children, and willingly devote themselves entirely to them; they seem never to be bored.

For them the days must come and go without distinction. Their fleeting beauty leaves them imperceptibly; they grow fat, they grow thin, wrinkled, and gaunt; the years pass and their life proceeds without change. They do not think, they do not live: they merely exist, and they die, and that is the end of it. I suppose they are as happy as any one else. After all, taking it from one point of view, it matters very little what sort of life one leads, there are so many people in the world, such millions have come and gone, such millions will come and go. If an individual makes no use of his hour what does it signify? He is only one among countless hordes. In the existence of these handsome creatures, so passionate and yet so apathetic, there are no particular pleasures beside the simple joys of sense, but on the other hand, beyond the inevitable separations of death, there are no outstanding griefs. They propagate their species, and that, perhaps, is the only quite certain duty that human beings have.

XVII

The Dance

Cervantes said that there was never born a Spanish woman but she was made to dance; and he might have added that in the South, at all events, most men share the enviable faculty. The dance is one of the most characteristic features of Andalusia, and as an amusement rivals in popularity even the bull-fight. The Sevillans dance on every possible occasion, and nothing pleases them more than the dexterity of professionals. Before a company has been assembled half an hour some one is bound to suggest that a couple should show their skill; room is quickly made, the table pushed against the wall, the chairs drawn back, and they begin. Even when men are alone in a tavern, drinking wine, two of them will often enough stand up to tread a seguidilla. On a rainy day it is the entertainment that naturally recommends itself.

Riding through the villages round Seville on Sundays it delighted me to see little groups making a circle about the house doors, in the middle of which were dancing two girls in bright-coloured clothes, with roses in their hair. A man seated on a broken chair was twanging a guitar, the surrounders beat their hands in time and the dancers made music with their castanets. Sometimes on a feast-day I came across a little band, arrayed in all its best, that had come into the country for an afternoon's diversion, and sat on the grass in the shade of summer or in the wintry sun. Whenever Andalusians mean to make merry some one will certainly bring a guitar, or if not the girls have their castanets; and though even these are wanting and no one can be induced to sing, a rhythmical clapping of hands will be sufficient accompaniment, and the performers will snap their fingers in lieu of castanets.

It is charming then to see the girls urge one another to dance; each vows with much dramatic gesture that she cannot, calling the Blessed Virgin to witness that she has strained her ankle and has a shocking cold. But some youth springs up and volunteers, inviting a particular damsel to join him. She is pushed forward, and the couple take their places. The man carefully puts down his cigarette, jams his broad-brimmed hat on his head, buttons his short coat and arches his back! The spectators cry: 'Ole!' The girl passes an arranging hand over her hair. The measure begins. The pair stand opposite one another, a yard or so distant, and foot it in accordance with one another's motions. It is not a thing of complicated steps, but, as one might expect from its Moorish origin, of movements of the body. With much graceful swaying from side to side the executants approach and retire, and at the middle of the dance change positions. It finishes with a great clapping of hands, the maiden sinks down among her friends and begins violently to fan herself, while her partner, with a great affectation of nonchalance, takes a seat and relights his cigarette.

And in the music-halls the national dances are, with the national songs, the principal attraction. Seville possesses but one of these establishments; it is a queer place, merely the patio of a private house, with a stage at one end, in which chairs and tables have been placed. On holiday nights it is crammed with students, with countrymen and artisans, with the general riff-raff of the town, and with women of no particular reputation. Now and then appears a gang of soldiers, giving a peculiar note with the uniformity of their brown holland suits; and occasionally a couple of British sailors come sauntering in with fine self-assurance, their fair hair and red cheeks contrasting with the general swartness. You pay no entrance money, but your refreshment costs a real—which is twopence ha'penny; and for that you may enjoy not only a cup of coffee or a glass of manzanilla, but an evening's entertainment. As the night wears on the heat is oven-like, and the air is thick and grey with the smoke of countless cigarettes.

The performance consists of three 'turns' only, and these are repeated every hour. The company boasts generally of a male singer, a female singer, and of the corps de ballet, which is made up of six persons. Spain is the stronghold of the out-of-date, and I suppose it alone preserves the stiff muslin ballet-skirts which delighted our fathers. To see half-a-dozen dancers thus attired in a remote Andalusian music-hall is so entirely unexpected that it quite takes the breath away. But by the time the traveller reaches Seville he must be used to disillusion, and he must be ingenuous indeed if he expects the Spaniards to have preserved their national costume for the most national of their pastimes. Yet the dances are still Spanish; and even if the pianoforte has ousted the guitar, the castanets give, notwithstanding, a characteristic note which the aggressive muslin and the pink, ill-fitting tights cannot entirely destroy.

52

But I remember one dancer who was really a great artist. She was ill-favoured, of middle age, thin; but every part of her was imbued with grace, expressive, from the tips of her toes to the tips of her fingers. The demands of the public sometimes forced upon her odious ballet-skirts, sometimes she wasted her talent on the futilities of skirt-dancing; but chiefly she loved the national measures, and her phenomenal leanness made her only comfortable in the national dress. She travelled from place to place in Spain with another woman whom she had taught to dance, and whose beauty she used cleverly as a foil to her own uncomeliness; and so wasted herself in these low resorts, earning hardly sufficient to keep body and soul together. I wish I could remember her name.

When she began to dance you forgot her ugliness; her gaunt arms gained shape, her face was transfigured, her dark eyes flashed, and her mouth and smile said a thousand eloquent things. Even the nape of her neck, which in most women has no significance, with her was expressive. A consummate actress, she exhibited all her skill in the bolero, which represents a courtship; she threw aside the castanets and wrapped herself in a mantilla, while her companion, dressed as a man, was hidden in a capa. The two passed one another, he trying to see the lady's face, which she averted, but not too strenuously; he pursued, she fled, but not too rapidly. Dropping his cloak, the lover attacked with greater warmth, while alternately she repelled and lured him on. At last she too cast away the mantilla. They seized the castanets and danced round one another with all manner of graceful and complicated evolutions, making love, quarrelling, pouting, exhibiting every variety of emotion. The dance grew more passionate, the steps flew faster, till at last, with the music, both stopped suddenly dead still. This abrupt cessation is one of the points most appreciated by a Spanish audience. 'Ole!' they cry,'bien parado!'

But when, unhampered by a partner, this nameless, exquisite dancer gave full play to her imagination, there was no end to the wildness of her fancy, to the intricacy and elaboration of her measures, to the gay audacity of her movements. She performed a hundred feats, each more difficult than the other—and all impossible to describe.

Then, between Christmas and Lent, at midnight on Saturdays and Sundays, the tables and the chairs are cleared away for the masked ball; and you will see the latest mode of Spanish dance. The women are of the lowest possible class; some, with a kind of savage irony, disguised as nuns, others in grotesque dominos of their own devising; but most wear every-day clothes with great shawls draped about them. The men are of a corresponding station, and through the evening wear their broad-brimmed hats. On the stage is a brass band, which plays one single tune till day-break, and to that one single measure is danced—the habanera.

In this alone may people take part as in any round dance. The couples hold one another in the very tightest embrace, the lady clasping her arms round her partner's neck, while he places both his about her waist. They go round the room very slowly, immediately behind one another; it is a kind of straight polka, with a peculiar, rhythmic swaying of the body; the feet are not lifted off the floor, and you do not turn at all. The highest gravity is preserved throughout, and the whole performance is—well, very oriental.

XVIII

A Feast Day

I arrived in Seville on the Eve of the Immaculate Conception. All day people had been preparing to celebrate the feast, decorating their houses with great banners of blue and white; and at night the silent, narrow streets had a strange appearance, for in every window were lighted candles, throwing around them a white, unusual glare; they looked a little like the souls of infants dead. All day the bells of a hundred churches had been ringing, half drowned by the rolling peals of the Giralda.

It had been announced that the archbishop would himself officiate at the High Mass in the Blessed Virgin's honour; and early in the morning the cathedral steps were crowded with black-robed women, making their way to the great sacristy where was to be held the service. I joined the throng, and entering through the darkness of the porch, was almost blinded by the brilliant altar, upon which stood a life-sized image of the Virgin, surrounded by a huge aureole, with great bishops, all of silver, on either side. It was ablaze with the light of many candles, so that the nave was thrown into deep shadow, and the kneeling women were scarcely visible.

The canons in the choir listlessly droned their prayers. At last the organ burst forth, and a long procession slowly came into the chapel, priests in white and blue, the colours of the Virgin, four bishops in mitres, the archbishop with his golden crozier; and preceding them all, in odd contrast, the beadle in black, with a dark periwig, bearing a silver staff. From the choir in due order they returned to the altar, headed this time by three pairs of acolytes, bearing great silver candlesticks, and by incense-burners, that filled the church with rich perfume.

When the Mass was finished, a young dark man in copious robes of violet ascended the pulpit and muttered a text. He waited an instant to collect himself, looking at the congregation; then turning to the altar began a passionate song of praise to the Blessed Virgin, unsoiled by original sin. He described her as in a hundred pictures the great painter of the Immaculate Conception has portrayed her— a young and graceful maid, clothed in a snowy gown of ample folds, with an azure cloak, a maid mysteriously pure; her hair, floating on the shoulders in luxurious ringlets, was an aureole more glorious than the silver rays which surrounded the great image; her dark eyes, with their languid lashes, her mouth, with the red lips, expressed a beautiful and immaculate virtue. It might have been some earthly woman of whom the priest spoke, one of those Andalusians that knelt below him, flashing quick glances at the gallant who negligently leaned against a pillar.

The archbishop sat on his golden throne—a thin, small man with a wrinkled face, with dead and listless eyes; in his gorgeous vestments he looked hardly human, he seemed a puppet, sitting stilly. At the end of the sermon he went back to the altar, and in his low, broken voice read the prayers. And then turning towards the great congregation he gave the plenary absolution, for which the Pope's Bull had been read from the pulpit steps.

In the afternoon, when the sun was going down behind the Guadalquivir, over the plain, I went again to the cathedral. The canons in the choir still droned their chant in praise of the Blessed Virgin, and in the greater darkness the altar shone more magnificently. The same procession filed through the nave, some priests were in black, some in violet, some in the Virgin's colours; but this time the archbishop wore gorgeous robes of scarlet, and as he knelt at the altar his train spread to the chancel steps. From the side appeared ten boys and knelt before the altar, and stood in two lines facing one another. They were dressed like pages of the seventeenth century, with white stockings and breeches, and a doublet of blue and silver, holding in their hands hats with long feathers. The archbishop, kneeling in front of the throne, buried his face in his hands.

A soft melody, played by violins and 'cellos, broke the silence, and presently the ten pages began to sing:

Los cielos y la tierra alaben al Señor
Con imnos de alabanza que inflamen al Señor[1].

---

[1] I believe there is no definite explanation of this ceremony, and the legend told me by an ancient priest that it was invented during the Moorish

It was a curious, old-fashioned music, reminding one a little of the quiet harmonies of Gluck. Then, putting on their hats, the pages danced, continuing their song; they wound in and out of one another, gravely footing it, swaying to and fro with the music very slowly. The measure was performed with the utmost reverence. Now and then the chorus came, and the fresh boys' voices, singing in unison, filled the church with delightful melody. And still the old archbishop prayed, his face buried in his hands.

The boys ceased to sing, but continued the dance, marking the time now with castanets, and the mundane instrument contrasted strangely with the glittering altar and with the kneeling priests. I wondered of what the archbishop thought, kneeling so humbly—of the boys dancing before the altar, fresh and young? Was he thinking of their white souls darkening with the sins of the world, or of the troubles, the disillusionments of life, and the decrepitude? Or was it of himself—did he think of his own youth, so long past, so hopelessly gone, or did he think that he was old and worn, and of the dark journey before him, and of the light that seemed so distant? Did he regret his beautiful Seville with the blue sky, and the orange-trees bowed down with their golden fruit? He seemed so small and weak, overwhelmed in his gorgeous robes.

Again the ten boys repeated their song and dance and their castanets, and with a rapid genuflection disappeared.

The archbishop rose painfully from his knees and ascended to the altar. A priest held open a book before him, and another lighted the printed page with a candle; he read out a prayer. Then, kneeling down, he bent very low, as though he felt himself unworthy to behold the magnificence of the Queen of Heaven. The people fell to their knees, and a man's voice burst forth—Ave Maria, gratia plena;

---

dominion so that Christian services might be held under cover of a social gathering—intruding Muslims would be told merely that people were there assembled to see boys dance and to listen to their singing—is more picturesque than probable. Rather does it seem analogous with the leaping of David the King before the Ark of Jehovah, when he danced before the Lord with all his might, girt with a linen Ephod; and this, if I may hazard an opinion, was with a view to amuse a deity apt to be bored or languid, just as Nautch girls dance to this day before the idols of the Hindus, and tops are spun before Krishna to divert him.

waves of passionate sound floated over the worshippers, upwards, towards heaven. And from the Giralda, the Moorish tower, the Christian bells rang joyfully. The archbishop turned towards the people; and when in his thin, broken voice he gave the benediction, one thought that no man in his heart felt such humility as the magnificent prince of the Church, Don Marcelo Spinola y Maestre, Archbishop of Seville.

The people flocked out quickly, and soon only a few devout penitents remained. A priest came, waving censers before the altar, and thick volumes of perfume ascended to the Blessed Virgin. He disappeared, and one by one the candles were extinguished. The night crept silently along the church, and the silver image sank into the darkness; at last two candles only were left on the altar, high up, shining dimly.

Outside the sky was still blue, bespattered with countless stars.

XIX

The Giralda

The Christian bells rang joyfully from the Moorish tower, the great old bells christened with holy oil, el Cantor the Singer, la Gorda the Great, San Miguel. I climbed the winding passage till I came to the terrace where stood the ringers, and as they pulled their ropes the bells swung round on their axles, completing a circle, with deafening clamour. The din was terrific, so that the solid masonry appeared to shake, and I felt the vibrations of the surrounding air. It was a strange sensation to shout as loud as possible and hear no sound issue from my mouth.

The Giralda, with its Moorish base and its Christian belfry, is a symbol of Andalusia. There is in the Ayuntamiento an old picture of the Minaret built by Djâbir the Moor, nearly one hundred feet shorter than the completed tower, but surmounted by a battlemented platform on which are huge brazen balls and an iron standard. These were overthrown by an earthquake, and later, when the discoveries of Christopher Columbus had poured unmeasured riches into Seville, the Chapter commissioned Hernan Ruiz to add a belfry to the Moorish base. Hernan Ruiz nearly ruined the mosque at Cordova, but here he was entirely successful. Indeed it is extraordinary that the two parts should be joined in such admirable harmony. It is impossible to give in words an idea of the slender grace of the Giralda, it does not look a thing of bricks and mortar, it is so straight and light that it reminds one vaguely of some beautiful human thing. The great height is astonishing, there is no buttress or projection to break the very long straight line as it rises, with a kind of breathless speed, to the belfry platform. And then the renaissance building begins, ascending still more, a sort of filigree work, excessively rich, and elegant beyond all praise. It is surmounted by a female figure of bronze, representing Faith and veering with every breeze, and the artist has surrounded his work with the motto: Nomen Domini Fortissima Turris.

But the older portion gains another charm from the Moorish windows that pierce it, one above the other, with horseshoe arches;

and from the arabesque network with which the upper part is diapered, a brick trellis-work against the brick walls, of the most graceful and delicate intricacy. The Giralda is almost toylike in the daintiness of its decoration. Notwithstanding its great size it is a masterpiece of exquisite proportion. At night it stands out with strong lines against the bespangled sky, and the lights of the watchers give it a magic appearance of some lacelike tower of imagination; but on high festivals it is lit with countless lamps, and then, as Richard Ford puts it, hangs from the dark vault of heaven like a brilliant chandelier.

I looked down at Seville from above. A Spanish town wears always its most picturesque appearance thus seen, but it is never different; the patios glaring with whitewash, the roofs of brown and yellow tiles, and the narrow streets, winding in unexpected directions, narrower than ever from such a height and dark with shade, so that they seem black rivulets gliding stealthily through the whiteness. Looking at a northern city from a tall church tower all things are confused with one another, the slate roofs join together till it is like a huge uneven sea of grey; but in Seville the atmosphere is so limpid, the colour so brilliant, that every house is clearly separated from its neighbour, and sometimes there appears to be between them a preternatural distinctness. Each stands independently of any other; you might suppose yourself in a strange city of the Arabian Nights where a great population lived in houses crowded together, but invisibly, so that each person fancied himself in isolation.

Immediately below was the Cathedral and to remind you of Cordova, the Court of Oranges; but here was no sunny restfulness, nor old-world quiet. The Court is gloomy and dark, and the trim rows of orange-trees contrast oddly with the grey stone of the Cathedral, its huge porches, and the flamboyant exuberance of its decoration. The sun never shines in it and no fruit splash the dark foliage with gold. You do not think of the generations of priests who have wandered in it on the summer evenings, basking away their peaceful lives in the sunshine; but rather of the busy merchants who met there in the old days when it was still the exchange of Seville, before the Lonja was built, to discuss the war with England, or the fate of ships bringing gold from America. At one end of the court is an old stone pulpit from which preached St. Francis of Borga and St. Vincent Ferrer and many an unknown monk besides. Then it was thronged with multi-coloured crowds, with townsmen, soldiers and great noblemen, when the faith was living and strong; and the preacher, with all the gesture and the impassioned rhetoric of a Spaniard, poured out burning words of hate for Jew and Moor and Heretic, so that the listeners panted and a veil of blood passed before their eyes; or else uttered so eloquent a song in praise of the Blessed Virgin, immaculately conceived, that strong men burst into tears at the recital of her perfect beauty.

XX

The Cathedral of Seville

Your first impression when you walk round the cathedral of Seville, noting with dismay the crushed cupolas and unsightly excrescences, the dinginess of colour, is not enthusiastic. It was built by German architects without a thought for the surrounding houses, brilliantly whitewashed, and the blue sky, and it proves the incongruity of northern art in a southern country; but even lowering clouds and mist could lend no charm to the late Gothic of Santa Maria de la Sede.

The interior fortunately is very different. Notwithstanding the Gothic groining, as you enter from the splendid heat of noonday, (in the Plaza del Triunfo the sun beats down and the houses are more dazzling than snow,) the effect is thoroughly and delightfully Spanish. Light is very fatal to devotion and the Spaniards have been so wise as to make their churches extremely dark. At first you can see nothing. Incense floats heavily about you, filling the air, and the coolness is like a draught of fresh, perfumed water. But gradually the church detaches itself from the obscurity and you see great columns, immensely lofty. The spaces are large and simple, giving an impression of vast room; and the choir, walled up on three sides, in the middle of the nave as in all Spanish cathedrals, by obstructing the view gives an appearance of almost unlimited extent. To me it seems that in such a place it is easier to comprehend the majesty wherewith man has equipped himself. Science offers only thoughts of human insignificance; the vastness of the sea, the terror of the mountains, emphasise the fact that man is of no account, ephemeral as the leaves of summer. But in those bold aisles, by the pillars rising with such a confident pride towards heaven, it is almost impossible not to feel that man indeed is god-like, lord of the earth; and that the great array of nature is builded for his purpose.

Typically Spanish also is the decoration, and very rich. The choir-stalls are of carved wood, florid and exuberant like the Spanish imagination; the altars gleam with gold; pictures of saints are framed by golden pillars carved with huge bunches of grapes and fruit and fantastic leaves. I was astounded at the opulence of the treasure; there were gorgeous altars of precious metal, great saints of silver, caskets of gold, monstrances studded with rare stones, crosses and crucifixes. The vestments were of unimaginable splendour: there were two hundred copes of all ages and of every variety, fifty of each colour, white for Christmas and Easter, red for Corpus Christi, blue for the Immaculate Conception, violet for Holy Week; there were the special copes of the Primate, copes for officiating bishops, copes for dignitaries from other countries and dioceses. They were of the richest velvet and satin, heavily embroidered with gold, many with saints worked in silk, so heavy that it seemed hardly possible for a man to bear them.

In the Baptistery, filling it with warm light, is the San Antonio of Murillo, than which no picture gives more intensely the religious emotion. The saint, tall and meagre, beautiful of face, looks at the Divine Child hovering in a golden mist with an ecstasy that is no longer human.

It is interesting to consider whether an artist need feel the sentiment he desires to convey. Certainly many pictures have been painted under the influence of profound feeling which leave the spectator entirely cold, and it is probable enough that the early Italians felt few of the emotions which their pictures call forth. We know that the masterpieces of Perugino, so moving, so instinct with religious tenderness, were very much a matter of pounds, shillings and pence. But Luis de Vargas, on the other hand, daily humbled himself by scourging and by wearing a hair shirt, and Vicente Joanes prepared himself for a new picture by communion and confession; so that it is impossible to wonder at the rude and savage ardour of their work. And the impression that may be gathered of Murillo from his pictures is borne out by the study of his grave and simple life. He had not the turbulent piety of the other two, but a calm and sweet devotion, which led him to spend long hours in church, meditating. He, at any rate, felt all that he expressed.

I do not know a church that gives the religious sentiment more completely than Seville Cathedral. The worship of the Spaniards is sombre, full-blooded, a thing of dark rich colours; it requires the heaviness of incense and that overloading of rococo decoration. It is curious that notwithstanding their extreme similarity to the Neapolitans, the Andalusians should in their faith differ so entirely. Of course, in Southern Italy religion is as full of superstition—an adoration of images in which all symbolism is lost and only the gross idol remains; but it is a gayer and a lighter thing than in Spain. Most characteristic of this is the difference between the churches; and with Santa Maria de la Sede may well be contrasted the Neapolitan Santa Chiara, with its great windows, so airy and spacious, sparkling with white and gold. The paintings are almost frolicsome. It is like a ballroom, a typical place of worship for a generation that had no desire to pray, but strutted in gaudy silks and ogled over pretty fans, pretending to discuss the latest audacity of Monsieur Arouet de Voltaire.

XXI

The Hospital of Charity

The Spaniards possess to the fullest degree the art of evoking devout emotions, and in their various churches may be experienced every phase of religious feeling. After the majestic size and the solemn mystery of the Cathedral, nothing can come as a greater contrast than the Church of the Hermandad de la Caredad. It was built by don Miguel de Mañara, who rests in the chancel, with the inscription over him: 'Aqui jacen los huesos y ceñizas del peor hombre que ha habido en el mundo; ruegan por el'—'Here lie the bones and ashes of the worst man that has ever been in the world; pray for him.' But like all Andalusians he was a braggart; for a love of chocolate, which appears to have been his besetting sin, is insufficient foundation for such a vaunt: a vice of that order is adequately punished by the corpulence it must occasion. However, legend, representing don Miguel as the most dissolute of libertines, is more friendly. The grave sister who escorts the visitor relates that one day in church don Miguel saw a beautiful nun, and undaunted by her habit, made amorous proposals. She did not speak, but turned to look at him, whereupon he saw the side of her face which had been hidden from his gaze, and it was eaten away by a foul and loathsome disease, so that it seemed more horrible than the face of death. The gallant was so terrified that he fainted, and afterwards the face haunted him, the face of matchless beauty and of revolting decay, so that he turned from the world. He devoted his fortune to rebuilding the hospital and church of the Brotherhood of Charity, whose chief office it was to administer the sacraments to those condemned to death and provide for their burial, and was eventually received into their Order.

It was in the seventeenth century that Mañara built his church, and consequently rococo holds sway with all its fantasies. It is small, without aisles or chapels, and the morbid opulence of the decoration gives it a peculiar character. The walls are lined with red damask, and the floor carpeted with a heavy crimson carpet; it gives the sensation of a hothouse, or, with its close odours, of a bedchamber transformed into a chapel for the administration of the last sacrament. The atmosphere is unhealthy: one pants for breath.

At one end, taking up the entire wall, is a reredos by Pedro Roldan, of which the centrepiece is an elaborate 'Deposition in the Tomb,' with numerous figures coloured to the life. It is very fine in its mingling of soft, rich hues and flamboyant realism. The artist has revelled in the opportunity for anguish of expression that his subject afforded, but has treated it with such a passionate seriousness that, in his grim, fierce way, he does not fail to be impressive. The frame is of twisted golden pillars, supported by little naked angels, and decorated with grapes and vine-leaves. Above and at the sides are great saints in carved wood, and angels with floating drapery.

Murillo was on terms of intimacy with don Miguel de Mañara, and like him a member of the Hermandad. For his friend he painted some of his most famous pictures, which by the subdued ardour of their colour, by their opulent tones, harmonise most exquisitely with the church. Marshal Soult, with a fine love of art that was profitable, carried off several of them, and their empty frames stare at one still. But before that, when they were all in place, the effect must have been of unique magnificence.

It must be an extraordinary religion that flourishes in such a place, an artificial faith that needs heat like tropical plants, that desires unnatural vows. It breathes of neurotic emotions with its damask-covered walls, with its carpet that deadens the footfall, its sombre, gorgeous pictures. The sweet breeze of heaven never enters there, nor the sunlight; the air is languid with incense; one is oppressed by a strange, heavy silence. In such a church sins must be fostered for the morbid pleasure of confession. One can imagine that the worshippers in that overloaded atmosphere would see strange visions, voluptuous and mystical; the Blessed Mary and the Saints might gain visible and palpable flesh, and the devil would not be far off. There the gruesome imaginings of Valdes Leal are a fitting decoration. Every one knows that grim picture of a bishop in episcopal robes, eaten by worms, his flesh putrefying, which led Murillo to say: 'Leal, you make me hold my nose,' and the other answered: 'You have taken all the flesh and left me nought but the bones.' Elsewhere, by the same master, there is a painting that suggests, with greater poignancy to my mind because less brutally, the thoughts evoked by the more celebrated work, and since it seems to complete the ideas awakened by this curious chapel, I mention it here.

It represents a priest at the altar, saying his mass, and the altar after the Spanish fashion is sumptuous with gilt and florid carving. He wears a magnificent cope and a surplice of exquisite lace, but he wears them as though their weight were more than he could bear; and in the meagre, trembling hands, and in the white, ashen face, in the dark hollowness of the eyes and in the sunken cheeks, there is a bodily corruption that is terrifying. The priest seems to hold together with difficulty the bonds of the flesh, but with no eager yearning of the soul to burst its prison, only with despair; it is as if the Lord Almighty had forsaken him, and the high heavens were empty of their solace. All the beauty of life appears forgotten, and there is nothing in the world but decay. A ghastly putrefaction has attacked already the living man; the worms of the grave, the piteous horror of mortality, and the darkness before him offer nought but fear, and what soul is there to rise again! Beyond, dark night is seen and a turbulent sea, the dark night of the soul of which the mystics write, and the troublous sea of life whereon there is no refuge for the weary and the sick at heart.

Then, if you would study yet another phase of the religious sentiment, go to the Museo, where are the fine pictures that Murillo painted for the Capuchin Monastery. You will see all the sombreness of Spanish piety, the savage faith, dissolved into ineffable love. Religion has become a wonderful tenderness, in which passionate human affection is inextricably mingled with god-like adoration. Murillo, these sensual forms quivering with life, brought the Eternal down to earth, and gave terrestrial ardour to the apathy of an impersonal devotion; that, perhaps, is why to women he has always been the most fascinating of painters. In the Madonna de la Servilleta—painted on a napkin for the cook of the monastery—the child is a simple, earthly infant, fresh and rosy, with wide-open, wondering eyes and not a trace of immortality. I myself saw a common woman of the streets stand before this picture with tears running down her cheeks.

'Corazon de mi alma!' she said, 'Heart of my soul! I could cover his little body with kisses.'

She smiled, but could hardly restrain her sobs. The engrossing love of a mother for her child seemed joined in miraculous union with the worship of a mortal for his God.

Murillo had neither the power nor the desire to idealise his models.

The saints of these great pictures, St. Francis of Assisi, St. Felix of Cantalicio, St. Thomas of Villanueva, are monks and beggars such as may to this day be seen in the streets of Seville. St. Felix is merely an old man with hollow cheeks and a grey, ragged beard; but yet as he clasps the child in his arms with eager tenderness, he is transfigured by a divine ecstasy: his face is radiant with the most touching emotion. And St. Antony of Padua, in another picture, worships the infant God with a mystic adoration, which, notwithstanding the realism of the presentment, lifts him far, far above the earth.

XXII

Gaol

I was curious to see the prison in Seville. Gruesome tales had been told me of its filth and horror, and the wretched condition of the prisoners; I had even heard that from the street you might see them pressing against the barred windows with arms thrust through, begging the passer-by for money or bread. Mediæval stories recurred to my mind and the clank of chains trailed through my imagination.

I arranged to be conducted by the prison doctor, and one morning soon after five set out to meet him. My guide informed me by a significant gesture that his tendencies were—bibulous, and our meeting-place was a tavern; but when we arrived they told us that don Felipe—such was his name—had been taken his morning dram and gone; however, if we went to another inn we should doubtless find him. But there we heard he had not yet arrived, he was not due till half-past five. To pass the time we drank a mouthful of aguardiente and smoked a cigarette, and eventually the medico was espied in the distance. We went towards him—a round, fat person with a red face and a redder nose, somewhat shabbily dressed.

He looked at me pointedly and said:

'I'm dry. Vengo seco.'

It was a hint not to be neglected, and we returned to the tavern where don Felipe had his nip.

'It's very good for the stomach,' he assured me.

We sallied forth together, and as we walked he told me the number of prisoners, the sort of crimes for which they were detained—ranging from man-slaughter to petty larceny—and finally, details of his own career. He was an intelligent man, and when we came to the prison door insisted on drinking my health.

The prison is an old convent, and it is a little startling to see the church façade, with a statue of the Madonna over the central porch. At the steps a number of women stood waiting with pots and jars and handkerchiefs full of food for their relatives within; and when the doctor appeared several rushed up to ask about a father or a son that lay sick. We went in and there was a melodramatic tinkling of keys and an unlocking of heavy doors.

The male prisoners, the adults, were in the patio of the convent, where in olden days the nuns had wandered on summer evenings, watering their roses. The iron door was opened and shut behind us; there was a movement of curiosity at the sight of a stranger, and many turned to look at me. Such as had illnesses came to the doctor, and he looked at their tongues and felt their pulse, giving directions to an assistant who stood beside him with a note-book. Don Felipe was on excellent terms with his patients, laughing and joking; a malingerer asked if he could not have a little wine because his throat was sore; the doctor jeered and the man began to laugh; they bandied repartees with one another.

There were about two hundred in the patio, and really they did not seem to have so bad a time. There was one large group gathered round a man who read a newspaper aloud; it was Monday morning, and all listened intently to the account of a bull-fight on the previous day, bursting into a little cry of surprise and admiration on hearing that the matador had been caught and tossed. Others lay by a pillar playing draughts for matches, while half a dozen more eagerly watched, giving unsolicited advice with much gesticulation. The draught-board consisted of little squares drawn on the pavement with chalk, and the pieces were scraps of white and yellow paper. One man sat cross-legged by a column busily rolling cigarettes; he had piles of them by his side arranged in packets, which he sold at one penny each; it was certainly an illegal offence, because the sale of tobacco is a government monopoly, but if you cannot break the laws in prison where can you break them? Others occupied themselves by making baskets or nets. But the majority did nothing at all, standing about, sitting when they could, with the eternal cigarette between their lips; and the more energetic watched the blue smoke curl into the air. Altogether a very happy family!

Nor did they seem really very criminal, more especially as they wore no prison uniform, but their own clothes. I saw no difference between them and the people I met casually in the street. They were just very ordinary citizens, countrymen smelling of the soil, labouring men, artisans. Their misfortune had been only to make too free a use of their long curved knives or to be discovered taking something over which another had prior claims. But in Andalusia every one is potentially as criminal, which is the same as saying that these jail-birds were estimable persons whom an unkind fate and a mistaken idea of justice had separated for a little while from their wives and families.

I saw two only whose aspect was distinctly vicious. One was a tall fellow with shifty eyes, a hard thin mouth, a cruel smile, and his face was really horrible. I asked the doctor why he was there. Don Felipe, without speaking, made the peculiar motion of the fingers which signifies robbery, and the man seeing him repeated it with a leer. I have seldom seen a face that was so utterly repellent, so depraved and wicked: I could not get it out of my head, and for a long time saw before me the crafty eyes and the grinning mouth. Obviously the man was a criminal born who would start thieving as soon as he was out of prison, hopelessly and utterly corrupt. But it was curious that his character should be marked so plainly on his face; it was a danger-signal to his fellows, and one would have thought the suspicion it aroused must necessarily keep him virtuous. It was a countenance that would make a man instinctively clap his hand to his pocket.

The other was a Turk, a huge creature, with dark scowling face and prominent brows; he made a singular figure in his bright fez and baggy breeches, looking at his fellow prisoners with a frown of hate.

But the doctor had finished seeing his patients and the iron door was opened for us to go out. We went upstairs to the hospital, a long bare ward, terribly cheerless. Six men, perhaps, lay in bed, guarded by two warders; one old fellow with rheumatism groaning in agony, two others dazed and very still, with high fever. We walked round quickly, don Felipe as before mechanically looking at their tongues and feeling their pulse, speaking a word to the assistant and moving on. The windows were shut and there was a horrid stench of illness and drugs and antiseptics.

We went through long corridors to the female side, and meanwhile the assistant told the doctor that during the night a woman had been confined. Don Felipe sat down in an office to write a certificate.

'What a nuisance these women are!' he said. 'Why can't they wait till they get out of prison? How is it?'

'It was still-born.'

'Pero, hombre,' said the doctor crossly. 'Why didn't you tell me that before? Now I shall have to write another certificate. This one's no good.'

He tore it up and painfully made out a second with the slow laborious writing of a man unused to holding a pen.

Then we marched on and came to another smaller patio where the females were. They were comparatively few, not more than twenty or thirty; and when we entered a dark inner-room to see the woman who was ill they all trooped in after us—all but one. They stood round eagerly telling us of the occurrence.

'Don't make such a noise, por Dios! I can't hear myself speak,' said the doctor.

The woman was lying on her back with flushed cheeks, her eyes staring glassily. The doctor asked a question, but she did not answer. She began to cry, sobbing from utter weakness in a silent, unrestrained way. On a table near her, hidden by a cloth, lay the dead child.

We went out again into the patio. The sun was higher now and it was very warm, the blue sky shone above us without a cloud. The prisoners returned to their occupations. One old hag was doing a younger woman's hair; I noticed that even for Spain it was beautiful, very thick, curling, and black as night. The girl held a carnation in her hand to put in front of the comb when the operation was completed. Another woman suckled a baby, and several tiny children were playing about happily, while their mothers chatted to one another, knitting.

But there was one, markedly different from the others, who sat alone taking no notice of the scene. It was she who remained in the patio when the rest followed us into the sick room, a gipsy, tall and gaunt, with a skin of the darkest yellow. Her hair was not elaborately arranged as that of her companions, but plainly done, drawn back stiffly from the forehead. She sat there, erect and motionless, looking at the ground with an unnatural stare, silent. They told me she never spoke a word nor paid attention to the women in the court. She might have been entirely alone. She never altered her position, but sat there, sphinx-like, in that attitude of stony grief. She was a stranger among the rest, and her bronzed face, her silence gave a weird impression; she seemed to recall the burning deserts of the East and an endless past.

At last we came out, and the heavy iron door was closed behind us. What a relief it was to be in the street again, to see the sun and the trees, and to breathe the free air! A cart went by with a great racket, drawn by three mules, and the cries of the driver as he cracked his whip were almost musical; a train of donkeys passed; a man trotted by on a brown shaggy cob, his huge panniers filled with glowing vegetables, green and red, and in a corner was a great bunch of roses. I took long breaths of the free air, I shook myself to get rid of those prison odours.

I offered don Felipe refreshment and we repaired to a dram-shop immediately opposite. Two women were standing there.

'Ole!' said the doctor to an old toothless hag with a vicious leer. 'What are you doing here? You've not been in for some time.'

She laughed and explained that she was come to fetch her friend, a young woman, who had been released that morning. The doctor nodded to her, asking how long she had been in gaol.

'Two years and nine months,' she said.

And she began to laugh hysterically with tears streaming down her cheeks.

'I don't know what I'm doing,' she cried. 'I can't understand it.'

She looked into the street with wild, yearning eyes; everything seemed to her strange and new.

'I haven't seen a tree for nearly three years,' she sobbed.

But the hag was pressing the doctor to drink with her; he accepted without much hesitation, and gallantly proposed her health.

'What are you going to do?' he said to the younger woman, she was hardly more than a girl. 'You'd better not hang about in Seville or you'll get into trouble again.'

'Oh no,' she said, 'I'm going to my village—mi pueblo—this afternoon. I want to see my husband and my child.'

Don Felipe turned to me and asked what I thought of the Seville prison. I made some complimentary reply.

'Are English prisons like that?' he asked.

I said I did not think so.

'Are they better?'

I shrugged my shoulders.

'I'm told,' he said, 'that two years' hard labour in an English prison kills a man.'

'The English are a great nation,' I replied.

'And a humane one,' he added, with a bow and a smile.

I bade him good-morning.

XXIII

Before the Bull-fight

If all Andalusians are potential gaol-birds they are also potential bull-fighters. It is impossible for foreigners to realise how firmly the love of that pastime is engrained in all classes. In other countries the gift that children love best is a box of soldiers, but in Spain it is a miniature ring with tin bulls, picadors on horseback and toreros. From their earliest youth boys play at bull-fighting, one of them taking the bull's part and charging with the movements peculiar to that animal, while the rest make passes with their coats or handkerchiefs. Often, to increase the excitement of the game, they have two horns fixed on a piece of wood. You will see them playing it at every street corner all day long, and no amusement can rival it; with the result that by the time a boy is fifteen he has acquired considerable skill in the exercise, and a favourite entertainment then is to hire a bull-calf for an afternoon and practise with it. Every urchin in Andalusia knows the names of the most prominent champions and can tell you their merits.

The bull-fight is the national spectacle; it excites Spaniards as nothing else can, and the death of a famous torero is more tragic than the loss of a colony. Seville looks upon itself as the very home and centre of the art. The good king Ferdinand VII.—as precious a rascal as ever graced a throne—founded in Seville the first academy for the cultivation of tauromachy, and bull-fighters swagger through the Sierpes in great numbers and the most faultless costume.

There are only five great bull-fights in a year at Seville, namely, on Easter day, on the three days of the fair, and on Corpus Christi. But during the summer novilladas are held every Sunday, with bulls of three years old and young fighters. Long before an important corrida there is quite an excitement in the town. Gaudy bills are posted on the walls with the names of the performers and the proprietor of the bulls; crowds stand round reading them breathlessly, discussing with one another the chances of the fray; the papers give details and forecasts as in England they do for the better cause of horse-racing! And the journeyings of the matador are announced as exactly as with us the doings of the nobility and gentry.

The great matador, Mazzantini or Guerrita, arrives the day before the fight, and perhaps takes a walk in the Sierpes. People turn to look at him and acquaintances shake his hand, pleased that all the world may know how friendly they are with so great a man. The hero himself is calm and gracious. He feels himself a person of merit, and cannot be unconscious that he has a fortune of several million pesetas bringing in a reasonable interest. He talks with ease and assurance, often condescends to joke, and elegantly waves his hand, sparkling with diamonds of great value.

Many persons have described a bull-fight, but generally their emotions have overwhelmed them so that they have seen only part of one performance, and consequently have been obliged to use an indignant imagination to help out a very faulty recollection. This is my excuse for giving one more account of an entertainment which can in no way be defended. It is doubtless vicious and degrading; but with the constant danger, the skill displayed, the courage, the hair-breadth escapes, the catastrophes, it is foolish to deny that any pastime can be more exciting.

The English humanity to animals is one of the best traits of a great people, and they justly thank God they are not as others are. Can anything more horrid be imagined than to kill a horse in the bull-ring, and can any decent hack ask for a better end when he is broken down, than to be driven to death in London streets or to stand for hours on cab ranks in the rain and snow of an English winter? The Spaniards are certainly cruel to animals; on the other hand, they never beat their wives nor kick their children. From the dog's point of view I would ten times sooner be English, but from the woman's—I have my doubts. Some while ago certain papers, anxious perhaps to taste the comfortable joys of self-righteousness, turned their attention to the brutality of Spaniards, and a score of journalists wrote indignantly of bull-fights. At the same time, by a singular chance, a prize-fighter was killed in London, and the Spanish papers printed long tirades against the gross, barbaric English. The two sets of writers were equally vehement, inaccurate and flowery; but what seemed most remarkable was that each side evidently felt quite unaffected horror and disgust for the proceedings of the other. Like persons of doubtful character inveighing against the vices of the age, both were so carried away by moral enthusiasm as to forget that there was anything in their own histories which made this virtuous fury a little absurd. There is really a good deal in the point of view.

XXIV

Corrida de Toros—I

On the day before a bull-fight all the world goes down to Tablada to see the bulls. Youth and beauty drive, for every one in Seville of the least pretension to gentility keeps a carriage; the Sevillans, characteristically, may live in houses void of every necessity and comfort, eating bread and water, but they will have a carriage to drive in the paseo. You see vehicles of all kinds, from the new landau with a pair of magnificent Andalusian horses, or the strange omnibus drawn by mules, typical of Southern Spain, to the shabby victoria, with a broken-down hack and a decrepit coachman.

Tablada is a vast common without the town, running along the river side, and here all manner of cattle are kept throughout the year. But the fighting bulls are brought from their respective farms the morning before the day of battle, and each is put in an enclosure with its attendant oxen. The crowd looks eagerly, admiring the length of horn, forecasting the fight.

The handsome brutes remain there till midnight, when they are brought to the ring and shut in little separate boxes till the morrow. The encierro, as it is called, is an interesting sight. The road has been palisaded and the bulls are driven along by oxen. It is very curious to wait in the darkness, in the silence, under the myriad stars of the southern night. Your ear is astrung to hear the distant tramp; the waiting seems endless. A sound is heard and every one runs to the side; but nothing follows, and the waiting continues. Suddenly the stillness is broken by tinkling bells, the oxen; and immediately there is a tramp of rushing hoofs. Three men on horseback gallop through the entrance, and on their heels the cattle; the riders turn sharply round, a door is swung to behind them, and the oxen, with the bulls in their midst, pound through the ring.

The doors are opened two hours before the performance. Through the morning the multitude has trooped to the Plaza San Fernando to buy tickets, and in the afternoon all Seville wends its way towards the ring. The road is thronged with people, they walk in dense crowds, pushing one another to get out of the way of broken-down shays that roll along filled with enthusiasts. The drivers crack their whips, shouting: 'Un real, un real a los Toros!'[2] The sun beats down and the sky is intensely blue. It is very hot, already people are blowing and panting, boys sell fans at a halfpenny each. 'Abanicos a perra chica!'[3]

When you come near the ring the din is tremendous; the many vendors shout their wares, middlemen offer tickets at double the usual price, friends call to one another. Now and then is a quarrel, a quick exchange of abuse as one pushes or treads upon his neighbour; but as a rule all are astonishingly good-natured. A man, after a narrow escape from being run over, will shout a joke to the driver, who is always ready with a repartee. And they surge on towards the entrance. Every one is expectant and thrilled, the very air seems to give a sense of exhilaration. The people crowd in like ants. All things are gay and full of colour and life.

A picador passes on horseback in his uncouth clothes, and all turn to look at him.

And in the ring itself the scene is marvellous. On one side the sun beats down with burning rays, and there, the seats being cheaper, notwithstanding the terrific heat people are closely packed. There is a perpetual irregular movement of thousands of women's fans fluttering to and fro. Opposite, in the shade, are nearly as many persons, but of better class. Above, in the boxes sit ladies in mantillas, and when a beautiful woman appears she is often greeted with a burst of applause, which she takes most unconcernedly. When at last the ring is full, tier above tier crammed so that not a place is vacant, it gives quite an extraordinary emotion. The serried masses cease then to be a collection of individuals, but gain somehow a corporate unity; you realise, with a kind of indeterminate fear, the many-headed beast of savage instincts and of ruthless might. No crowd is more picturesque than the Spanish, and the dark masculine costume vividly contrasts with the bright colours of the women, with flowers in their hair and mantillas of white lace.

But also the tremendous vitality of it all strikes you. Late arrivals

---

[2] 'Twopence-halfpenny to the Bulls.'
[3] "Fans, one halfpenny each!"

walk along looking for room, gesticulating, laughing, bandying jokes; vendors of all sorts cry out their goods: the men who sell prawns, shrimps, and crabs' claws from Cadiz pass with large baskets: 'Bocas, bocas!'

The water sellers with huge jars: 'Agua, quien quiere agua? Agua!'[4] The word sings along the interminable rows. A man demands a glass and hands down a halfpenny; a mug of sparkling water is sent up to him. It is deliciously cool.

The sellers of lottery tickets, offering as usual the first prize: 'Premio gordo, quien quiere el premio gordo';[5] or yelling the number of the ticket: 'Who wants number seventeen hundred and eighty-five for three pesetas?'

And the newsboys add to the din: 'Noticiero! Porvenir!' Later on arrives the Madrid paper: 'Heraldo! Heraldo!'

Lastly the men with stacks of old journals to use as seats: 'A perra chica, dos periodicos a perra chica!'[6]

Suddenly there is a great clapping of hands, and looking up you find the president has come; he is supported by two friends, and all three, with comic solemnity, wear tall hats and frock coats. They bow to the public. Bull-fighting is the only punctual thing in Spain, and the president arrives precisely as the clock strikes half-past four. He waves a handkerchief, the band strikes up, a door is opened, and the fighters enter. First come the three matadors, the eldest in the middle, the next on his right, and the youngest on the left; they are followed by their respective cuadrillas, the banderilleros, the capeadors, the picadors on horseback, and finally the chulos, whose duty it is to unsaddle dead horses, attach the slaughtered bull to the team of mules, and perform other minor offices. They advance, gorgeous in their coloured satin and gold embroidery, bearing a cloak peculiarly folded over the arm; they walk with a kind of swinging motion, as ordained by the convention of a century. They bow to the president, very solemnly. The applause is renewed. They retire to the side, three picadors take up their places at some distance from one another on the right of the

---

4 'Water, who wants water? Water!'
5 'The first prize, who wants the first prize?'
6 'One halfpenny, two papers for one halfpenny.'

door from which issues the bull. The alguaciles, in black velvet, with peaked and feathered hats, on horseback, come forward, and the key of the bull's den is thrown to them. They disappear. The fighters meanwhile exchange their satin cloaks for others of less value. There is another flourish of trumpets, the gates are opened for the bull.

Then comes a moment of expectation, every one is trembling with excitement. There is perfect silence. All eyes are fixed on the open gate.

XXV

Corrida de Toros—II

One or two shouts are heard, a murmur passes through the people, and the bull emerges—shining, black, with massive shoulders and fine horns. It advances a little, a splendid beast conscious of its strength, and suddenly stops dead, looking round. The toreros wave their capes and the picadors flourish their lances, long wooden spikes with an iron point. The bull catches sight of a horse, and lowering his head, bears down swiftly upon it. The picador takes firmer hold of his lance, and when the brute reaches him plants the pointed end between its shoulders; at the same moment the senior matador dashes forward and with his cloak distracts the bull's attention. It wheels round and charges; he makes a pass; it goes by almost under his arm, but quickly turns and again attacks. This time the skilful fighter receives it backwards, looking over his shoulder, and again it passes. There are shouts of enthusiasm from the public. The bull's glossy coat is stained with red.

A second picador comes forward, and the bull charges again, but furiously now, exerting its full might. The horse is thrown to the ground and the rider, by an evil chance, falls at the bull's very feet.

It cannot help seeing him and lowers its head; the people catch their breath; many spring instinctively to their feet; here and there is a woman's frightened cry; but immediately a matador draws the cape over its eyes and passionately the bull turns on him. Others spring forward and lift the picador: his trappings are so heavy that he cannot rise alone; he is dragged to safety and the steed brought back for him. One more horseman advances, and the bull with an angry snort bounds at him; the picador does his best, but is no match for the giant strength. The bull digs its horns deep into the horse's side and lifts man and beast right off the ground; they fall with a heavy thud, and as the raging brute is drawn off, blood spurts from the horse's flank. The chulos try to get it up; they drag on the reins with shouts and curses, and beat it with sticks. But the wretched creature, wounded to the death, helplessly lifts its head. They see it is useless and quickly remove saddle and bridle, a man comes with a short dagger called the puntilla, which he drives into its head, the horse falls on its side, a quiver passes through its body, and it is dead. The people are shouting with pleasure; the bull is a good one. The first picador comes up again and the bull attacks for the fourth time, but it has lost much strength, and the man drives it off. It has made a horrible gash in the horse's belly, and the entrails protrude, dragging along the ground. The horse is taken out.

The president waves his handkerchief, the trumpets sound, and the first act of the drama is over.

The picadors leave the ring and the banderilleros take their darts, about three feet long, gay with decorations of coloured paper. While they make ready, others play with the bull, gradually tiring it: one throws aside his cape and awaits the charge with folded arms; the bull rushes at him, and the man without moving his feet twists his body away and the savage brute passes on. There is a great burst of applause for a daring feat well done.

Each matador has two banderilleros, and it is proper that three pairs of these darts should be placed. One of them steps to within speaking distance of the animal, and holding a banderilla in each hand lifted above his head, stamps his foot and shouts insulting words. The bull does not know what this new thing is, but charges blindly; at the same moment the man runs forward, and passing, plants the two darts between the shoulders. If they are well placed there is plentiful hand-clapping; no audience is so liberal of applause for skill or courage, none so intolerant of cowardice or stupidity; and with equal readiness it will yell with delight or hiss and hoot and whistle. The second banderillero comes forward to plant his pair; a third is inserted and the trumpets sound for the final scene.

This is the great duel between the single man and the bull. The matador advances, sword in hand, with the muleta, the red cloth for the passes, over his arm. Under the president's box he takes off his hat, and with fine gesture makes a grandiloquent speech, wherein he vows either to conquer or to die: the harangue is finished with a wheel round and a dramatic flinging of his hat to attendants on the other side of the barrier. He pensively walks forward. All eyes are upon him—and he knows it. He motions his companions to stand back and goes close to the bull. He is quite alone, with his life in his hands—a slender figure, very handsome in the gorgeous costume glittering with fine gold. He arranges the muleta over a little stick, so that it hangs down like a flag and conceals his sword. Then quite solemnly he walks up to the bull, holding the red rag in his left hand. The bull watches suspiciously, suddenly charges, and the muleta is passed over its head; the matador does not move a muscle, the bull turns and stands quite motionless. Another charge, another pass. And so he continues, making seven or eight of various sorts, to the growing approbation of the public. At last it is time to kill. With great caution he withdraws the sword; the bull looks warily. He makes two or three passes more and walks round till he gets the animal into proper position: the forefeet must be set squarely on the ground. 'Ora! Ora!' cry the people. 'Now! Now!' The bull is well placed. The matador draws the sword back a little and takes careful aim. The bull rushes, and at the same moment the man makes one bound forward and buries the sword to the hilt between the brute's shoulders. It falls to its knees and rolls over.

Then is a perfect storm of applause; and it is worth while to see fourteen thousand people wild with delight. The band bursts into joyous strains, and the mules come galloping in, gaily caparisoned; a rope is passed round the dead beast, and they drag it away. The matador advances to the president's box and bows, while the shouting grows more frantic. He walks round, bowing and smiling, and the public in its enthusiasm throws down hats and cigars and sticks.

But there are no intervals to a bull-fight, and the picadors immediately reappear and take their places; the doors are flung open, and a second bull rushes forth. The matador still goes round bowing to the applause, elaborately unmindful of the angry beast.

Six animals are killed in an afternoon within two hours, and then the mighty audience troop out with flushed cheeks, the smell of blood strong in their nostrils.

XXVI

On Horseback

I had a desire to see something of the very heart of Andalusia, of that part of the country which had preserved its antique character, where railway trains were not, and the horse, the mule, the donkey were still the only means of transit. After much scrutiny of local maps and conversation with horse-dealers and others, I determined from Seville to go circuitously to Ecija, and thence return by another route as best I could. The district I meant to traverse in olden times was notorious for its brigands; even thirty years ago the prosperous tradesman, voyaging on his mule from town to town, was liable to be seized by unromantic outlaws and detained till his friends forwarded ransom, while ears and fingers were playfully sent to prove identity. In Southern Spain brigandage necessarily flourished, for not only were the country-folk in collusion with the bandits, but the very magistrates united with them to share the profits of lawless undertakings. Drastic measures were needful to put down the evil, and in a truly Spanish way drastic measures were employed. The Civil Guard, whose duty it was to see to the safety of the country side, had no confidence in the justice of Madrid, whither captured highwaymen were sent for trial; once there, for a few hundred dollars, the most murderous ruffian could prove his babe-like innocence, forthwith return to the scene of his former exploits and begin again. So they hit upon an expedient. The Civil Guards set out for the capital with their prisoner handcuffed between them; but, curiously enough, in every single case the brigand had scarcely marched a couple of miles before he incautiously tried to escape, whereupon he was, of course, promptly shot through the back. People noticed two things: first, that the clothes of the dead man were often singed, as if he had not escaped very far before he was shot down; that only proved his guardians' zeal. But the other was stranger: the two Civil Guards, when after a couple of hours they returned to the town, as though by a mysterious premonition they had known the bandit would make some rash attempt, invariably had waiting for them an excellent hot dinner.

The only robber of importance who avoided such violent death was the chief of a celebrated band who, when captured, signed a declaration that he had not the remotest idea of escaping, and insisted on taking with him to Madrid his solicitor and a witness. He reached the capital alive, and having settled his little affairs with benevolent judges, turned to a different means of livelihood, and eventually, it is said, occupied a responsible post in the Government. It is satisfactory to think that his felonious talents were not in after-life entirely wasted.

It was the beginning of March when I started. According to the old proverb, the dog was already seeking the shade: En Marzo busca la sombra el perro; the chilly Spaniard, loosening the folds of his capa, acknowledged that at mid-day in the sun it was almost warm. The winter rains appeared to have ceased; the sky over Seville was cloudless, not with the intense azure of midsummer, but with a blue that seemed mixed with silver. And in the sun the brown water of the Guadalquivir glittered like the scales on a fish's back, or like the burnished gold of old Moorish pottery.

I set out in the morning early, with saddle-bags fixed on either side and poncho strapped to my pommel. A loaded revolver, though of course I never had a chance to use it, made me feel pleasantly adventurous. I walked cautiously over the slippery cobbles of the streets, disturbing the silence with the clatter of my horse's shoes. Now and then a mule or a donkey trotted by, with panniers full of vegetables, of charcoal or of bread, between which on the beast's neck sat perched a man in a short blouse. I came to the old rampart of the town, now a promenade; and at the gate groups of idlers, with cigarettes between their lips, stood talking.

An hospitable friend had offered lodging for the night and food; after which, my ideas of the probable accommodation being vague, I expected to sleep upon straw, for victuals depending on the wayside inns. I arrived at the Campo de la Cruz, a tiny chapel which marks the same distance from the Cathedral as Jesus Christ walked to the Cross; it is the final boundary of Seville.

Immediately afterwards I left the high-road, striking across country to Carmona. The land was already wild; on either side of the bridle-path were great wastes of sand covered only by palmetto. The air was cool and fresh, like the air of English country in June when it has rained through the night; and Aguador, snorting with pleasure, cantered over the uneven ground, nimbly avoiding holes and deep

85

ruts with the sure-footedness of his Arab blood. An Andalusian horse cares nothing for the ground on which he goes, though it be hard and unyielding as iron; and he clambers up and down steep, rocky precipices as happily as he trots along a cinder-path.

I passed a shepherd in a ragged cloak and a broad-brimmed hat, holding a crook. He stared at me, his flock of brown sheep clustered about him as I scampered by, and his dog rushed after, barking.

'Vaya Usted con Dios!'

I came to little woods of pine-trees, with long, thin trunks, and the foliage spreading umbrella-wise; round them circled innumerable hawks, whose nests I saw among the branches. Two ravens crossed my path, their wings heavily flapping.

The great charm of the Andalusian country is that you seize romance, as it were, in the act. In northern lands it is only by a mental effort that you can realise the picturesque value of the life that surrounds you; and, for my part, I can perceive it only by putting it mentally in black and white, and reading it as though between the covers of a book. Once, I remember, in Brittany, in a distant corner of that rock-bound coast, I sat at midnight in a fisherman's cottage playing cards by the light of two tallow candles. Next door, with only a wall between us, a very old sailor lay dying in the great cupboard-bed which had belonged to his fathers before him; and he fought for life with the remains of that strenuous vigour with which in other years he had battled against the storms of the Atlantic. In the stillness of the night, the waves, with the murmur of a lullaby, washed gently upon the shingle, and the stars shone down from a clear sky. I looked at the yellow light on the faces of the players, gathered in that desolate spot from the four corners of the earth, and cried out: 'By Jove, this is romance!' I had never before caught that impression in the very making, and I was delighted with my good fortune.

The answer came quickly from the American: 'Don't talk bosh! It's your deal.'

But for all that it was romance, seized fugitively, and life at that moment threw itself into a decorative pattern fit to be remembered. It is the same effect which you get more constantly in Spain, so that the commonest things are transfigured into beauty. For in the cactus and the aloe and the broad fields of grain, in the mules with their wide panniers and the peasants, in the shepherds' huts and the straggling farm-houses, the romantic is there, needing no subtlety to be discovered; and the least imaginative may feel a certain thrill when he understands that the life he leads is not without its æsthetic meaning.

I rode for a long way in complete solitude, through many miles of this sandy desert. Then the country changed, and olive-groves in endless succession followed one another, the trees with curiously decorative effect were planted in long, even lines. The earth was a vivid red, contrasting with the blue sky and the sombre olives, gnarled and fantastically twisted, like evil spirits metamorphosed: in places they had sown corn, and the young green enhanced the shrill diversity of colour. With its clear, brilliant outlines and its lack of shadow, the scene reminded one of a prim pattern, such as in Jane Austen's day young gentlewomen worked in worsted. Sometimes I saw women among the trees, perched like monkeys on the branches, or standing below with large baskets; they were extraordinarily quaint in the trousers which modesty bade them wear for the concealment of their limbs when olive-picking. The costume was so masculine, their faces so red and weather-beaten, that the yellow handkerchief on their heads was really the only means of distinguishing their sex.

But the path became more precipitous, hewn from the sandstone, and so polished by the numberless shoes of donkeys and of mules that I hardly dared walk upon it; and suddenly I saw Carmona in front of me—quite close.

XXVII

By the Road—I

The approach to Carmona is a very broad, white street, much too wide for the cottages which line it, deserted; and the young trees planted on either side are too small to give shade. The sun beat down with a fierce glare and the dust rose in clouds as I passed. Presently I came to a great Moorish gateway, a dark mass of stone, battlemented, with a lofty horseshoe arch. People were gathered about it in many-coloured groups, I found it was a holiday in Carmona, and the animation was unwonted; in a corner stood the hut of the Consumo, and the men advanced to examine my saddle-bags. I passed through, into the town, looking right and left for a parador, an hostelry whereat to leave my horse. I bargained for the price of food and saw Aguador comfortably stalled; then made my way to the Nekropolis where lived my host. There are many churches in Carmona, and into one of these I entered; it had nothing of great interest, but to a certain degree it was rich, rich in its gilded woodwork and in the brocade that adorned the pillars; and I felt that these Spanish churches lent a certain dignity to life: for all the careless flippancy of Andalusia they still remained to strike a nobler note. I forgot willingly that the land was priest-ridden and superstitious, so that a Spaniard could tell me bitterly that there were but two professions open to his countrymen, the priesthood and the bull-ring. It was pleasant to rest in that cool and fragrant darkness.

My host was an archæologist, and we ate surrounded by broken earthenware, fragmentary mosaics, and grinning skulls. It was curious afterwards to wander in the graveyard which, with indefatigable zeal, he had excavated, among the tombs of forgotten races, letting oneself down to explore the subterranean cells. The paths he had made in the giant cemetery were lined with a vast number of square sandstone boxes which had contained human ashes; and now, when the lid was lifted, a green lizard or a scorpion darted out. From the hill I saw stretched before me the great valley of the Guadalquivir: with the squares of olive and of ploughed field, and the various greens of the corn, it was like a vast, multi-coloured carpet. But later, with the sunset, black clouds arose, splendidly piled upon one another; and the twilight air was chill and grey. A certain sternness came over the olive-groves, and they might well have served as a reproach to the facile Andaluz; for their cold passionless green seemed to offer a warning to his folly.

At night my host left me to sleep in the village, and I lay in bed alone in the little house among the tombs; it was very silent. The wind sprang up and blew about me, whistling through the windows, whistling weirdly; and I felt as though the multitudes that had been buried in that old cemetery filled the air with their serried numbers, a vast, silent congregation waiting motionless for they knew not what. I recalled a gruesome fact that my friend had told me: not far from there, in tombs that he had disinterred the skeletons lay huddled spasmodically, with broken skulls and a great stone by the side; for when a man, he said, lay sick unto death, his people took him, and placed him in his grave, and with the stone killed him.

In the morning I set out again. It was five-and-thirty miles to Ecija, but a new high road stretched from place to place and I expected easy riding. Carmona stands on the top of a precipitous hill, round which winds the beginning of the road; below, after many zigzags, I saw its continuation, a straight white line reaching as far as I could see. In Andalusia, till a few years ago, there were practically no high roads, and even now they are few and bad. The chief communication from town to town is usually an uneven track, which none attempts to keep up, with deep ruts, and palmetto growing on either side, and occasional pools of water. A day's rain makes it a quagmire, impassable for anything beside the sure-footed mule.

I went on, meeting now and then a string of asses, their panniers filled with stones or with wood for Carmona; the drivers sat on the rump of the hindmost animal, for that is the only comfortable way to ride a donkey. A peasant trotted briskly by on his mule, his wife behind him with her arms about his waist. I saw a row of ploughs in a field; to each were attached two oxen, and they went along heavily, one behind the other in regular line. By the side of every pair a man walked bearing a long goad, and one of them sang a Malagueña, its monotonous notes rising and falling slowly. From time to time I passed a white farm, a little way from the road, invitingly cool in the heat; the sun began to beat down fiercely. The inevitable storks were perched on a chimney, by their big nest; and when they flew in front of me, with their broad white wings and their red legs against the blue sky, they gave a quaint impression of a Japanese screen.

A farmhouse such as this seems to me always a type of the Spanish impenetrability. I have been over many of them, and know the manner of their rooms and the furniture, the round of duties there performed and how the day is portioned out; but the real life of the inhabitants escapes me. My knowledge is merely external. I am conscious that it is the same of the Andalusians generally, and am dismayed because I know practically nothing more after a good many years than I learnt in the first months of my acquaintance with them. Below the superficial similarity with the rest of Europe which of late they have acquired, there is a difference which makes it impossible to get at the bottom of their hearts. They have no openness as have the French and the Italians, with whom a good deal of intimacy is possible even to an Englishman, but on the contrary an Eastern reserve which continually baffles me. I cannot realise their thoughts nor their outlook. I feel always below the grace of their behaviour the instinctive, primeval hatred of the stranger.

Gradually the cultivation ceased, and I saw no further sign of human beings. I returned to the desert of the previous day, but the land was more dreary. The little groves of pine-trees had disappeared, there were no olives, no cornfields, not even the aloe nor the wilder cactus; but on either side as far as the horizon, desert wastes, littered with stones and with rough boulders, grown over only by palmetto. For many miles I went, dismounting now and then to stretch my legs and sauntering a while with the reins over my shoulder. Towards mid-day I rested by the wayside and let Aguador eat what grass he could.

Presently, continuing my journey, I caught sight of a little hovel where the fir-branch over the door told me wine was to be obtained. I fastened my horse to a ring in the wall, and, going in, found an aged crone who gave me a glass of that thin white wine, produce of the last year's vintage, which is called Vino de la Hoja, wine of the leaf; she looked at me incuriously as though she saw so many people and they were so much alike that none repaid particular scrutiny. I tried to talk with her, for it seemed a curious life that she must lead, alone in that hut many miles from the nearest hamlet, with never a house in sight; but she was taciturn and eyed me now with something like suspicion. I asked for food, but with a sullen frown she answered that she had none to spare. I inquired the distance to Luisiana, a village on the way to Ecija where I had proposed to lunch, and shrugging her shoulders, she replied: 'How should I know!' I was about to go when I heard a great clattering, and a horseman galloped up. He dismounted and walked in, a fine example of the Andalusian countryman, handsome and tall, well-shaved, with close-cropped hair. He wore elaborately decorated gaiters, the usual short, close-fitting jacket, and a broad-brimmed hat; in his belt were a knife and a revolver, and slung across his back a long gun. He would have made an admirable brigand of comic-opera; but was in point of fact a farmer riding, as he told me, to see his novia, or lady-love, at a neighbouring farm.

I found him more communicative and in the politest fashion we discussed the weather and the crops. He had been to Seville.

'Che maravilla!' he cried, waving his fine, strong hands. 'What a marvel! But I cannot bear the town-folk. What thieves and liars!'

'Town-folk should stick to the towns,' muttered the old woman, looking at me somewhat pointedly.

The remark drew the farmer's attention more closely to me.

'And what are you doing here?' he asked.

'Riding to Ecija.'

'Ah, you're a commercial traveller,' he cried, with fine scorn. 'You foreigners bleed the country of all its money. You and the government!'

'Rogues and vagabonds!' muttered the old woman.

Notwithstanding, the farmer with much condescension accepted one of my cigars, and made me drink with him a glass of aguardiente.

We went off together. The mare he rode was really magnificent, rather large, holding her head beautifully, with a tail that almost swept the ground. She carried as if it were nothing the heavy Spanish saddle, covered with a white sheep-skin, its high triangular pommel of polished wood. Our ways, however, quickly diverged. I inquired again how far it was to the nearest village.

'Eh!' said the farmer, with a vague gesture. 'Two leagues. Three leagues. Quien sabe? Who knows? Adios!'

He put the spurs to his mare and galloped down a bridle-track. I, whom no fair maiden awaited, trotted on soberly.

XXVIII

By the Road—II

The endless desert grew rocky and less sandy, the colours duller. Even the palmetto found scanty sustenance, and huge boulders, strewn as though some vast torrent had passed through the plain, alone broke the desolate flatness. The dusty road pursued its way, invariably straight, neither turning to one side nor to the other, but continually in front of me, a long white line.

Finally in the distance I saw a group of white buildings and a cluster of trees. I thought it was Luisiana, but Luisiana, they had said, was a populous hamlet, and here were only two or three houses and not a soul. I rode up and found among the trees a tall white church, and a pool of murky water, further back a low, new edifice, which was evidently a monastery, and a posada. Presently a Franciscan monk in his brown cowl came out of the church, and he told me that Luisiana was a full league off, but that food could be obtained at the neighbouring inn.

The posada was merely a long barn, with an open roof of wood, on one side of which were half a dozen mangers and in a corner two mules. Against another wall were rough benches for travellers to sleep on. I dismounted and walked to the huge fireplace at one end, where I saw three very old women seated like witches round a brasero, the great brass dish of burning cinders. With true Spanish stolidity they did not rise as I approached, but waited for me to speak, looking at me indifferently. I asked whether I could have anything to eat.

'Fried eggs.'

'Anything else?'

The hostess, a tall creature, haggard and grim, shrugged her shoulders. Her jaws were toothless, and when she spoke it was difficult to understand. I tied Aguador to a manger and took off his saddle. The old women stirred themselves at last, and one brought a portion of chopped straw and a little barley. Another with the bellows blew on the cinders, and the third, taking eggs from a basket, fried them on the brasero. Besides, they gave me coarse brown bread and red wine, which was coarser still; for dessert the hostess went to the door and from a neighbouring tree plucked oranges.

When I had finished—it was not a very substantial meal—I drew my chair to the brasero and handed round my cigarette-case. The old women helped themselves, and a smile of thanks made the face of my gaunt hostess somewhat less repellent. We smoked a while in silence.

'Are you all alone here?' I asked, at length.

The hostess made a movement of her head towards the country. 'My son is out shooting,' she said, 'and two others are in Cuba, fighting the rebels.'

'God protect them!' muttered another.

'All our sons go to Cuba now,' said the first. 'Oh, I don't blame the Cubans, but the government.'

An angry light filled her eyes, and she lifted her clenched hand, cursing the rulers at Madrid who took her children. 'They're robbers and fools. Why can't they let Cuba go? It isn't worth the money we pay in taxes.'

She spoke so vehemently, mumbling the words between her toothless gums, that I could scarcely make them out.

'In Madrid they don't care if the country goes to rack and ruin so long as they fill their purses. Listen.' She put one hand on my arm. 'My boy came back with fever and dysentery. He was ill for months—at death's door—and I nursed him day and night. And almost before he could walk they sent him out again to that accursed country.'

The tears rolled heavily down her wrinkled cheeks.

Luisiana is a curious place. It was a colony formed by Charles III. of Spain with Germans whom he brought to people the desolate land; and I fancied the Teuton ancestry was apparent in the smaller civility of the inhabitants. They looked sullenly as I passed, and none gave the friendly Andalusian greeting. I saw a woman hanging clothes on the line outside her house; she had blue eyes and flaxen hair, a healthy red face, and a solidity of build which proved the purity of her northern blood. The houses, too, had a certain exotic quaintness; notwithstanding the universal whitewash of the South, there was about them still a northern character. They were prim and regularly built, with little plots of garden; the fences and the shutters were bright green. I almost expected to see German words on the post-office and on the tobacco-shop, and the grandiloquent Spanish seemed out of place; I thought the Spanish clothes of the men sat upon them uneasily.

The day was drawing to a close and I pushed on to reach Ecija before night, but Aguador was tired and I was obliged mostly to walk. Now the highway turned and twisted among little hills and it was a strange relief to leave the dead level of the plains: on each side the land was barren and desolate, and in the distance were dark mountains. The sky had clouded over, and the evening was grey and very cold; the solitude was awful. At last I overtook a pedlar plodding along by his donkey, the panniers filled to overflowing with china and glass, which he was taking to sell in Ecija. He wished to talk, but he was going too slowly, and I left him. I had hills to climb now, and at the top of each expected to see the town, but every time was disappointed. The traces of man surrounded me at last; again I rode among olive-groves and cornfields; the highway now was bordered with straggling aloes and with hedges of cactus.

At last! I reached the brink of another hill, and then, absolutely at my feet, so that I could have thrown a stone on its roofs, lay Ecija with its numberless steeples.

XXIX

Ecija

The central square, where are the government offices, the taverns, and a little inn, is a charming place, quiet and lackadaisical, its pale browns and greys very restful in the twilight, and harmonious. The houses with their queer windows and their balconies of wrought iron are built upon arcades which give a pleasant feeling of intimacy: in summer, cool and dark, they must be the promenade of all the gossips and the loungers. One can imagine the uneventful life, the monotonous round of existence; and yet the Andalusian blood runs in the people's veins. To my writer's fantasy Ecija seemed a fit background for some tragic story of passion or of crime.

I dined, unromantically enough, with a pair of commercial travellers, a post-office clerk, and two stout, elderly men who appeared to be retired officers. Spanish victuals are terrible and strange; food is even more an affair of birth than religion, since a man may change his faith, but hardly his manner of eating: the stomach used to roast meat and Yorkshire pudding rebels against Eastern cookery, and a Christian may sooner become a Buddhist than a beef-eater a guzzler of olla podrida. The Spaniards without weariness eat the same dinner day after day, year in, year out: it is always the same white, thin, oily soup; a dish of haricot beans and maize swimming in a revolting sauce; a nameless entrée fried in oil—Andalusians have a passion for other animals' insides; a thin steak, tough as leather and grilled to utter dryness; raisins and oranges. You rise from table feeling that you have been soaked in rancid oil.

My table-companions were disposed to be sociable. The travellers desired to know whether I was there to sell anything, and one drew from his pocket, for my inspection, a case of watch-chains. The officers surmised that I had come from Gibraltar to spy the land, and to terrify me, spoke of the invincible strength of the Spanish forces.

'Are you aware,' said the elder, whose adiposity prevented his outward appearance from corresponding with his warlike heart, 'Are you aware that in the course of history our army has never once been defeated, and our fleet but twice?'

He mentioned the catastrophes, but I had never heard of them; and Trafalgar was certainly not included. I hazarded a discreet inquiry, whereupon, with much emphasis, both explained how on that occasion the Spanish had soundly thrashed old Nelson, although he had discomfited the French.

'It is odd,' I observed, 'that British historians should be so inaccurate.'

'It is discreditable,' retorted my acquaintance, with a certain severity.

'How long did the English take to conquer the Soudan?' remarked the other, somewhat aggressively picking his teeth. 'Twenty years? We conquered Morocco in three months.'

'And the Moors are devils,' said the commercial traveller. 'I know, because I once went to Tangiers for my firm.'

After dinner I wandered about the streets, past the great old houses of the nobles in the Calle de los Caballeros, empty now and dilapidated, for every gentleman that can put a penny in his pocket goes to Madrid to spend it; down to the river which flowed swiftly between high banks. Below the bridge two Moorish mills, irregular masses of blackness, stood finely against the night. Near at hand they were still working at a forge, and I watched the flying sparks as the smith hammered a horseshoe; the workers were like silhouettes in front of the leaping flames.

At many windows, to my envy, couples were philandering; the night was cold and Corydon stood huddled in his cape. But the murmuring as I passed was like the flow of a rapid brook, and I imagined, I am sure, far more passionate and romantic speeches than ever the lovers made. I might have uttered them to the moon, but I should have felt ridiculous, and it was more practical to jot them down afterwards in a note-book. In some of the surrounding villages they have so far preserved the Moorish style as to have no windows within reach of the ground, and lovers then must take advantage of the aperture at the bottom of the door made for the domestic cat's particular convenience. Stretched full length on the

96

ground, on opposite sides of the impenetrable barrier, they can still whisper amorous commonplaces to one another. But imagine the confusion of a polite Spaniard, on a dark night, stumbling over a recumbent swain:

'My dear sir, I beg your pardon. I had no idea....'

In old days the disturbance would have been sufficient cause for a duel, but now manners are more peaceful: the gallant, turning a little, removes his hat and politely answers:

'It is of no consequence. Vaya Usted con Dios!'

'Good-night!'

The intruder passes and the beau endeavours passionately to catch sight of his mistress' black eyes.

Next day was Sunday, and I walked by the river till I found a plot of grass sheltered from the wind by a bristly hedge of cactus. I lay down in the sun, lazily watching two oxen that ploughed a neighbouring field.

I felt it my duty in the morning to buy a chap-book relating the adventures of the famous brigands who were called the Seven Children of Ecija; and this, somewhat sleepily, I began to read. It required a byronic stomach, for the very first chapter led me to a monastery where mass proceeded in memory of some victim of undiscovered crime. Seven handsome men appeared, most splendidly arrayed, but armed to the teeth; each one was every inch a brigand, pitiless yet great of heart, saturnine yet gentlemanly; and their peculiarity was that though six were killed one day seven would invariably be seen the next. The most gorgeously apparelled of them all, entering the sacristy, flung a purse of gold to the Superior, while a scalding tear coursed down his sunburnt cheek; and this he dried with a noble gesture and a richly embroidered handkerchief! In a whirlwind of romantic properties I read of a wicked miser who refused to support his brother's widow, of the widow herself, (brought at birth to a gardener in the dead of night by a mysterious mulatto,) and of this lady's lovely offspring. My own feelings can never be harrowed on behalf of a widow with a marriageable daughter, but I am aware that habitual readers of romance, like ostriches, will swallow anything. I was hurried to a subterranean chamber where the Seven Children, in still more elaborate garments, performed various dark deeds, smoked expensive Havanas, and seated on silken cushions, partook (like Freemasons) of a succulent cold collation.

The sun shone down with comfortable warmth, and I stretched my legs. My pipe was out and I refilled it. A meditative snail crawled up and observed me with flattering interest.

I grew somewhat confused. A stolen will was of course inevitable, and so were prison dungeons; but the characters had an irritating trick of revealing at critical moments that they were long-lost relatives. It must have been a tedious age when poor relations were never safely buried. However, youth and beauty were at last triumphant and villainy confounded, virtue was crowned with orange blossom and vice died a miserable death. Rejoicing in duty performed I went to sleep.

XXX

Wind and Storm

But next morning the sky was dark with clouds; people looked up dubiously when I asked the way and distance to Marchena, prophesying rain. Fetching my horse, the owner of the stable robbed me with peculiar callousness, for he had bound my hands the day before, when I went to see how Aguador was treated, by giving me with most courteous ceremony a glass of aguardiente; and his urbanity was then so captivating that now I lacked assurance to protest. I paid the scandalous overcharge with a good grace, finding some solace in the reflection that he was at least a picturesque blackguard, tall and spare, grey-headed, with fine features sharpened by age to the strongest lines; for I am always grateful to the dishonest when they add a certain æsthetic charm to their crooked ways. There is a proverb which says that in Ecija every man is a thief and every woman—no better than she should be: I was not disinclined to believe it.

I set out, guided by a sign-post, and the good road seemed to promise an easy day. They had told me that the distance was only six leagues, and I expected to arrive before luncheon. Aguador, fresh after his day's rest, broke into a canter when I put him on the green plot, which the old Spanish law orders to be left for cattle by the side of the highway. But after three miles, without warning, the road suddenly stopped. I found myself in an olive-grove, with only a narrow path in front of me. It looked doubtful, but there was no one in sight and I wandered on, trusting to luck.

Presently, in a clearing, I caught sight of three men on donkeys, walking slowly one after the other, and I galloped after to ask my way. The beasts were laden with undressed skins which they were taking to Fuentes, and each man squatted cross-legged on the top of his load. The hindermost turned right round when I asked my question and sat unconcernedly with his back to the donkey's head. He looked about him vaguely as though expecting the information I sought to be written on the trunk of an olive-tree, and scratched his head.

'Well,' he said, 'I should think it was a matter of seven leagues, but it will rain before you get there.'

'This is the right way, isn't it?'

'It may be. If it doesn't lead to Marchena it must lead somewhere else.'

There was a philosophic ring about the answer which made up for the uncertainty. The skinner was a fat, good-humoured creature, like all Spaniards intensely curious; and to prepare the way for inquiries, offered a cigarette.

'But why do you come to Ecija by so roundabout a way as Carmona, and why should you return to Seville by such a route as Marchena?'

His opinion was evidently that the shortest way between two places was also the best. He received my explanation with incredulity and asked, more insistently, why I went to Ecija on horseback when I might go by train to Madrid.

'For pleasure,' said I.

'My good sir, you must have come on some errand.'

'Oh yes,' I answered, hoping to satisfy him, 'on the search for emotion.'

At this he bellowed with laughter and turned round to tell his fellows.

'Usted es muy guason,' he said at length, which may be translated: 'You're a mighty funny fellow.'

I expressed my pleasure at having provided the skinners with amusement and bidding them farewell, trotted on.

I went for a long time among the interminable olives, grey and sad beneath the sullen clouds, and at last the rain began to fall. I saw a farm not very far away and cantered up to ask for shelter. An old woman and a labourer came to the door and looked at me very doubtfully; they said it was not a posada, but my soft words turned their hearts and they allowed me to come in. The rain poured down in heavy, oblique lines.

The labourer took Aguador to the stable and I went into the parlour, a long, low, airy chamber like the refectory of a monastery, with windows reaching to the ground. Two girls were sitting round the brasero, sewing; they offered me a chair by their side, and as the rain fell steadily we began to talk. The old woman discreetly remained away. They asked about my journey, and as is the Spanish mode, about my country, myself, and my belongings. It was a regular volley of questions I had to answer, but they sounded pleasanter in the mouth of a pretty girl than in that of an obese old skinner; and the rippling laughter which greeted my replies made me feel quite witty. When they smiled they showed the whitest teeth. Then came my turn for questioning. The girl on my right, prettier than her sister, was very Spanish, with black, expressive eyes, an olive skin, and a bunch of violets in her abundant hair. I asked whether she had a novio, or lover; and the question set her laughing immoderately. What was her name? 'Soledad—Solitude.'

I looked somewhat anxiously at the weather, I feared the shower would cease, and in a minute, alas! the rain passed away; and I was forced to notice it, for the sun-rays came dancing through the window, importunately, making patterns of light upon the floor. I had no further excuse to stay, and said good-bye; but I begged for the bunch of violets in Soledad's dark hair and she gave it with a pretty smile. I plunged again into the endless olive-groves.

It was a little strange, the momentary irruption into other people's lives, the friendly gossip with persons of a different tongue and country, whom I had never seen before, whom I should never see again; and were I not strictly truthful I might here lighten my narrative by the invention of a charming and romantic adventure. But if chance brings us often for a moment into other existences, it takes us out with equal suddenness so that we scarcely know whether they were real or mere imaginings of an idle hour: the Fates have a passion for the unfinished sketch and seldom trouble to unravel the threads which they have so laboriously entangled. The little scene brought another to my mind. When I was 'on accident duty' at St. Thomas's Hospital a man brought his son with a broken leg; it was hard luck on the little chap, for he was seated peacefully on the ground when another boy, climbing a wall, fell on him and did the damage. When I returned him, duly bandaged, to his father's arms, the child bent forward and put out his lips for a kiss, saying good-night with babyish pronunciation. The father and the attendant nurse laughed, and I, being young, was confused and blushed profusely. They went away and somehow or other I never

101

saw them again. I wonder if the pretty child, (he must be eight or ten now,) remembers kissing a very weary medical student, who had not slept much for several days, and was dead tired. Probably he has quite forgotten that he ever broke his leg. And I suppose no recollection remains with the pretty girl in the farm of a foreigner riding mysteriously through the olive-groves, to whom she gave shelter and a bunch of violets.

I came at last to the end of the trees and found then that a mighty wind had risen, which blew straight in my teeth. It was hard work to ride against it, but I saw a white town in the distance, on a hill; and made for it, rejoicing in the prospect. Presently I met some men shooting, and to make sure, asked whether the houses I saw really were Marchena.

'Oh no,' said one. 'You've come quite out of the way. That is Fuentes. Marchena is over there, beyond the hill.'

My heart sank, for I was growing very hungry, and I asked whether I could not get shelter at Fuentes. They shrugged their shoulders and advised me to go to Marchena, which had a small inn. I went on for several hours, battling against the wind, bent down in order to expose myself as little as possible, over a huge expanse of pasture land, a desert of green. I reached the crest of the hill, but there was no sign of Marchena, unless that was a tower which I saw very far away, its summit just rising above the horizon.

I was ravenous. My saddle-bags contained spaces for a bottle and for food; and I cursed my folly in stuffing them with such useless refinements of civilisation as hair-brushes and soap. It is possible that one could allay the pangs of hunger with soap; but under no imaginable circumstances with hair-brushes.

It was a tower in the distance, but it seemed to grow neither nearer nor larger; the wind blew without pity, and miserably Aguador tramped on. I no longer felt very hungry, but dreadfully bored. In that waste of greenery the only living things beside myself were a troop of swallows that had accompanied me for miles. They flew close to the ground, in front of me, circling round; and the wind was so high that they could scarcely advance against it.

I remembered the skinner's question, why I rode through the country when I could go by train. I thought of the Cheshire Cheese in Fleet Street, where persons more fortunate than I had that day eaten hearty luncheons. I imagined to myself a well-grilled steak with boiled potatoes, and a pint of old ale, Stilton! The smoke rose to my nostrils.

But at last, the Saints be praised! I found a real bridle-path, signs of civilisation, ploughed fields; and I came in sight of Marchena perched on a hill-top, surrounded by its walls. When I arrived the sun was setting finely behind the town.

XXXI

Two Villages

Marchena was all white, and on the cold windy evening I spent there, deserted of inhabitants. Quite rarely a man sidled past wrapped to the eyes in his cloak, or a woman with a black shawl over her head. I saw in the town nothing characteristic but the wicker-work frame in front of each window, so that people within could not possibly be seen; it was evidently a Moorish survival. At night men came into the eating-room of the inn, ate their dinner silently, and muffling themselves, quickly went out; the cold seemed to have killed all life in them. I slept in a little windowless cellar, on a straw bed which was somewhat verminous.

But next morning, as I looked back, the view of Marchena was charming. It stood on the crest of a green hill, surrounded by old battlements, and the sun shone down upon it. The wind had fallen, and in the early hour the air was pleasant and balmy. There was no road whatever, not even a bridle-track this time, and I made straight for Seville. I proposed to rest my horse and lunch at Mairena. On one side was a great plain of young corn stretching to the horizon, and on the other, with the same mantle of green, little hills, round which I slowly wound. The sun gave all manner of varied tints to the verdure—sometimes it was all emerald and gold, and at others it was like dark green velvet.

But the clouds in the direction of Seville were very black, and coming nearer I saw that it rained upon the hills. The water fell on the earth like a transparent sheet of grey. Soon I felt an occasional drop, and I put on my poncho.

The rain began in earnest, no northern drizzle, but a streaming downpour that soaked me to the skin. The path became marsh-like, and Aguador splashed along at a walk; it was impossible to go faster. The rain pelted down, blinding me. Then, oddly enough, for the occasion hardly warranted such high-flown thoughts, I felt suddenly the utter helplessness of man: I had never before realised with such completeness his insignificance beside the might of

Nature; alone, with not a soul in sight, I felt strangely powerless. The plain flaunted itself insolently in face of my distress, and the hills raised their heads with a scornful pride; they met the rain as equals, but me it crushed; I felt as though it would beat me down into the mire. I fell into a passion with the elements, and was seized with a desire to strike out. But the white sheet of water was senseless and impalpable, and I relieved myself by raging inwardly at the fools who complain of civilisation and of railway-trains; they have never walked for hours foot-deep in mud, terrified lest their horse should slip, with the rain falling as though it would never cease.

The path led me to a river; there was a ford, but the water was very high, and rushed and foamed like a torrent. Ignorant of the depth and mistrustful, I trotted up-stream a little, seeking shallower parts; but none could be seen, and it was no use to look for a bridge. I was bound to cross, and I had to risk it; my only consolation was that even if Aguador could not stand, I was already so wet that I could hardly get wetter. The good horse required some persuasion before he would enter; the water rushed and bubbled and rapidly became deeper; he stopped and tried to turn back, but I urged him on. My feet went under water, and soon it was up to my knees; then, absurdly, it struck me as rather funny, and I began to laugh; I could not help thinking how foolish I should look and feel on arriving at the other side, if I had to swim for it. But immediately it grew shallower; all my adventures tailed off thus unheroically just when they began to grow exciting, and in a minute I was on comparatively dry land.

I went on, still with no view of Mairena; but I was coming nearer. I met a group of women walking with their petticoats over their heads. I passed a labourer sheltered behind a hedge, while his oxen stood in a field, looking miserably at the rain. Still it fell, still it fell!

And when I reached Mairena it was the most cheerless place I had come across on my journey, merely a poverty-stricken hamlet that did not even boast a bad inn. I was directed from place to place before I could find a stable; I was soaked to the skin, and there seemed no shelter. At last I discovered a wretched wine-shop; but the woman who kept it said there was no fire and no food. Then I grew very cross. I explained with heat that I had money; it is true I was bedraggled and disreputable, but when I showed some coins, to prove that I could pay for what I bought, she asked unwillingly what

I required. I ordered a brasero, and dried my clothes as best I could by the burning cinders. I ate a scanty meal of eggs, and comforted myself with the thin wine of the leaf, sufficiently alcoholic to be exhilarating, and finally, with aguardiente regained my equilibrium.

But the elements were against me. The rain had ceased while I lunched, but no sooner had I left Mairena than it began again, and Seville was sixteen miles away. It poured steadily. I tramped up the hills, covered with nut-trees; I wound down into valleys; the way seemed interminable. I tramped on. At last from the brow of a hill I saw in the distance the Giralda and the clustering houses of Seville, but all grey in the wet; above it heavy clouds were lowering. On and on!

The day was declining, and Seville now was almost hidden in the mist, but I reached a road. I came to the first tavern of the environs; after a while to the first houses, then the road gave way to slippery cobbles, and I was in Seville. The Saints be praised!

XXXII

Granada

To go from Seville to Granada is like coming out of the sunshine into deep shadow. I arrived, my mind full of Moorish pictures, expecting to find a vivid, tumultuous life; and I was ready with a prodigal hand to dash on the colours of my admiration. But Granada is a sad town, grey and empty; its people meander, melancholy, through the streets, unoccupied. It is a tradeless place living on the monuments which attract strangers, and like many a city famous for stirring history, seems utterly exhausted. Granada gave me an impression that it wished merely to be left alone to drag out its remaining days in peace, away from the advance of civilisation and the fervid hurrying of progress: it seemed like a great adventuress retired from the world after a life of vicissitude, anxious only to be forgotten, and after so much storm and stress to be nothing more than pious. There must be many descendants of the Moors, but the present population is wan and lifeless. They are taciturn, sombre folk, with nothing in them of the chattering and vivacious creatures of Arab history. Indeed, as I wandered through the streets, it was not the Moors that engaged my mind, but rather Ferdinand of Arragon and Isabella of Castille. Their grim strength over-powered the more graceful shadows of Moordom; and it was only by an effort that I recalled Gazul and Musa, most gallant and amorous of Paynim knights, tilting in the square, displaying incredible valour in the slaughter of savage bulls. I thought of the Catholic Kings, in full armour, riding with clank of steel through the captured streets. And the snowy summits of the Sierra Nevada, dazzling sometimes under the sun and the blue sky, but more often veiled with mist and capped by heavy clouds, grim and terrifying, lent a sort of tragic interest to the scene; so that I felt those grey masses, with their cloak of white, (they seemed near enough to overwhelm one,) made it impossible for the town built at their very feet, to give itself over altogether to flippancy.

And for a while I found little of interest in Granada but the Alhambra. The gipsy quarter, with neither beauty, colour, nor even a touch of barbarism, is a squalid, brutal place, consisting of little dens built in the rock of the mountain which stands opposite the Alhambra. Worse than hovels, they are the lairs of wild beasts, fœtid and oppressive, inhabited by debased creatures, with the low forehead, the copper skin, and the shifty cruel look of the Spanish gipsy. They surround the visitor in their rags and tatters, clamouring for alms, and for exorbitant sums proposing to dance. Even in the slums of great cities I have not seen a life more bestial. I tried to imagine what sort of existence these people led. In the old days the rock-dwellings among the cactus served the gipsies for winter quarters only, and when the spring came they set off, scouring the country for something to earn or steal; but that is long ago. For two generations they have remained in these hovels—year in, year out—employed in shoeing horses, shearing, and the like menial occupations which the Spaniard thinks beneath his dignity. The women tell fortunes, or dance for the foreigner, or worse. It is a mere struggle for daily bread. I wondered whether in the spring-time the young men loved the maidens, or if they only coupled like the beasts. I saw one pair who seemed quite newly wed; for their scanty furniture was new and they were young. The man, short and squat, sat scowling, cross-legged on a chair, a cigarette between his lips. The woman was taller and not ill-made, a slattern; her hair fell dishevelled on her back and over her forehead; her dress was open, displaying the bosom; her apron was filthy. But when she smiled, asking for money, her teeth were white and regular, and her eyes flashed darkly. She was attractive in a heavy sensual fashion, attractive and at the same time horribly repellant: she was the sort of woman who might fetter a man to herself by some degrading, insuperable passion, the true Carmen of the famous story whom a man might at once love and hate; so that though she dragged him to hell in shame and in despair, he would never find the strength to free himself. But where among that bastard race was the splendid desire for freedom of their fathers, the love of the fresh air of heaven and the untrammeled life of the fields?

At first glance also the cathedral seemed devoid of charm. I suppose travellers seek emotions in the things they see, and often the more beautiful objects do not give the most vivid sensations. Painters complain that men of letters have written chiefly of second-rate pictures, but the literary sentiment is different from the artistic; and a masterpiece of Perugino may excite it less than a mediocre work of Guido Reni.

The cathedral of Granada is said by the excellent Fergusson to be the most noteworthy example in Europe of early Renaissance architecture; its proportions are evidently admirable, and it is designed and carried out according to all the canons of the art. 'Looking at its plan only,' he says, 'this is certainly one of the finest churches in Europe. It would be difficult to point out any other, in which the central aisle leads up to the dome, so well proportioned to its dimensions, and to the dignity of the high altar which stands under it.' But though I vaguely recognised these perfections, though the spacing appeared fine and simple, and the columns had a certain majesty, I was left more than a little cold. The whitewash with which the interior is coated gives an unsympathetic impression, and the abundant light destroys that mystery which the poorest, gaudiest Spanish church almost invariably possesses. In the Capilla de los Reyes are the elaborate monuments of the Catholic Kings, of their daughter Joan the Mad, and of Philip her husband; below, in the crypt, are four simple coffins, in which after so much grandeur, so much joy and sorrow, they rest. Indeed, for the two poor women who loved without requite, it was a life of pain almost unrelieved: it is a pitiful story, for all its magnificence, of Joan with her fiery passion for the handsome, faithless, worthless husband, and her mad jealousy; and of Isabella, with patient strength bearing every cross, always devoted to the man who tired of her quickly, and repaid her deep affection with naught but coldness and distrust.

Queen Isabella's sword and sceptre are shown in the sacristry, and in contrast with the implement of war a beautiful cope, worked with her royal hands. And her crown also may be seen, one of the few I have come across which might really become the wearer, of silver, a masterpiece of delicate craftsmanship.

But presently, returning to the cathedral and sitting in front of the high altar, I became at last conscious of its airy, restful grace. The chancel is very lofty. The base is a huge arcade which gives an effect of great lightness; and above are two rows of pictures, and still higher two rows of painted windows. The coloured glass throws the softest lights upon the altar and on the marble floor, rendering even quieter the low tints of the pictures. These are a series of illustrations of the life of the Blessed Virgin, painted by Alonzo Cano, a native of Valladolid, who killed his wife and came to Granada, whereupon those in power made him a prebendary. In the obscurity I could not see the paintings, but divined soft and pleasant things after the style of Murillo, and doubtless that was better than actually to see them. The pulpits are gorgeously carved in wood, and from the walls fly great angels with fine turbulence of golden drapery. And in the contrast of the soft white stone with the gold, which not even the most critical taste could complain was too richly spread, there is a delicate, fascinating lightness: the chancel has almost an Italian gaiety, which comes upon one oddly in the gloomy town. Here the decoration, the gilded virgins, the elaborate carving, do not oppress as elsewhere; the effect is too debonair and too refreshing. It is one colour more, one more distinction, in the complexity of the religious sentiment.

But if what I have said of Granada seems cold, it is because I did not easily catch the spirit of the place. For when you merely observe and admire some view, and if industrious make a note of your impression, and then go home to luncheon, you are but a vulgar tripper, scum of the earth, deserving the ridicule with which the natives treat you. The romantic spirit is your only justification; when by the comeliness of your life or the beauty of your emotion you have attained that, (Shelley when he visited Paestum had it, but Théophile Gautier, flaunting his red waistcoat tras los montes, was perhaps no better than a Cook's tourist,) then you are no longer unworthy of the loveliness which it is your privilege to see. When the old red brick and the green trees say to you hidden things, and the vega and the mountains are stretched before you with a new significance, when at last the white houses with their brown tiles, and the labouring donkey, and the peasant at his plough, appeal to you so as to make, as it were, an exquisite pattern on your soul, then you may begin to find excuses for yourself. But you may see places long and often before they are thus magically revealed to you, and for myself I caught the real emotion of Granada but once, when from the Generalife I looked over the valley, the Generalife in which are mingled perhaps more admirably than anywhere else in Andalusia all the charm of Arabic architecture, of running water, and of cypress trees, of purple flags and dark red roses. It is a spot, indeed, fit for the plaintive creatures of poets to sing their loves, for Paolo and Francesca, for Juliet and Romeo; and I am glad that there I enjoyed such an exquisite moment.

XXXIII

The Alhambra

From the church of San Nicolas, on the other side of the valley, the Alhambra, like all Moorish buildings externally very plain, with its red walls and low, tiled roofs, looks like some old charter-house. Encircled by the fresh green of the spring-time, it lies along the summit of the hill with an infinite, most simple grace, dun and brown and deep red; and from the sultry wall on which I sat the elm-trees and the poplars seemed very cool. Thirstily, after the long drought, the Darro, the Arab stream which ran scarlet with the blood of Moorish strife, wound its way over its stony bed among the hills; and beyond, in strange contrast with all the fertility, was the grey and silent grandeur of the Sierra Nevada. Few places can be more charming than the green wood in which stands the stronghold of the Moorish kings; the wind sighs among the topmost branches and all about is the sweet sound of running water; in spring the ground is carpeted with violets, and the heavy foliage gives an enchanting coldness. A massive gateway, flanked by watch-towers, forms the approach; but the actual entrance, offering no hint of the incredible magnificence within, is an insignificant door.

But then, then you are immediately transported to a magic palace, existing in some uncertain age of fancy, which does not seem the work of human hands, but rather of Jin, an enchanted dwelling of seven lovely damsels. It is barely conceivable that historical persons inhabited such a place. At the same time it explains the wonderful civilisation of the Moors in Spain, with their fantastic battles, their songs and strange histories; and it brings the Arabian Nights into the bounds of sober reality: after he has seen the Alhambra none can doubt the literal truth of the stories of Sinbad the Sailor and of Hasan of Bassorah.

From the terrace that overlooks the city you enter the Court of Myrtles—a long pool of water with goldfish swimming to and fro, enclosed by myrtle hedges. At the ends are arcades, borne by marble columns with capitals of surpassing beauty. It is very quiet and very restful; the placid water gives an indescribable sensation of delight, and at the end mirrors the slender columns and the decorated arches so that in reflection you see the entrance to a second palace, which is filled with mysterious, beautiful things. But in the Alhambra the imagination finds itself at last out of its depth, it cannot conjure up chambers more beautiful than the reality presents. It serves only to recall the old inhabitants to the deserted halls.

The Moors continually used inscriptions with great effect, and there is one in this court which surpasses all others in its oriental imagery, in praise of Mohammed V.: Thou givest safety from the breeze to the blades of grass, and inspirest terror in the very stars of heaven. When the shining stars quiver, it is through dread of thee, and when the grass of the field bends down it is to give thee thanks.

But it is the Hall of the Ambassadors which shows most fully the unparalleled splendour of Moorish decoration. It is a square room, very lofty, with alcoves on three sides, at the bottom of which are windows; and the walls are covered, from the dado of tiles to the roof, with the richest and most varied ornamentation. The Moorish workmen did not spare themselves nor economise their exuberant invention. One pattern follows another with infinite diversity. Even the alcoves, and there are nine, are covered each with different designs, so that the mind is bewildered by their graceful ingenuity. All kinds of geometrical figures are used, enlacing with graceful intricacy, intersecting, combining and dissolving; conventional foliage and fruit, Arabic inscriptions. An industrious person has counted more than one hundred and fifty patterns in the Hall of the Ambassadors, impressed with iron moulds on the moist plaster of the walls. The roof is a low dome of larch wood, intricately carved and inlaid with ivory and with mother-of-pearl; it has been likened to the faceted surface of an elaborately cut gem. The effect is so gorgeous that you are oppressed; you long for some perfectly plain space whereon to rest the eye; but every inch is covered.

Now the walls have preserved only delicate tints of red and blue, pale Wedgwood blues and faded terracottas, that make with the ivory of the plaster most exquisite harmonies; but to accord with the tiles, their brilliancy still undiminished, the colours must have been very bright. The complicated patterns and the gay hues reproduce the oriental carpets of the nomad's tent; for from the tent, it is said, (I know not with what justification,) all oriental architecture is derived. The fragile columns upon which rest masses of masonry

112

are, therefore, direct imitations of tent-poles, and the stalactite borders of the arches represent the fringe of the woven hangings. The Moorish architect paid no attention to the rules of architecture, and it has been well said that if they existed for him at all it was only that he might elaborately disregard them. His columns generally support nothing; his arcades, so delicately worked that they seem like carved ivory, are of the lightest wood and plaster.

And it is curious that there should be such durability in those dainty materials: they express well the fatalism of the luxurious Moor, to whom the past and future were as nothing, and the transient hour all in all; yet they have outlasted him and his conqueror. The Spaniard, inglorious and decayed, is now but the showman to this magnificence; time has seen his greatness come and go, as came and went the greatness of the Moor, but still, for all its fragility, the Alhambra stands hardly less beautiful. Travellers have always been astonished at the small size of the Alhambra, especially of the Court of Lions; for here, though the proportion is admirable the scale is tiny; and many have supposed that the Moors were of less imposing physique than modern Europeans. The Court is surrounded by exquisite little columns, singly, in twos, in threes, supporting horseshoe arches; and in the centre is that beautiful fountain, borne by twelve lions with bristly manes, standing very stiffly, whereon is the inscription: O thou who beholdest these lions crouching, fear not. Life is wanting to enable them to show their fury.

Indeed, their surroundings have such a delicate and playful grace that it is hard to believe the Moors had any of our strenuous, latter-day passions. Life must have been to them a masque rather than a tragi-comedy; and whether they belong to sober history or no, those contests of which the curious may read in the lively pages of Gines Perez de Hita accord excellently with the fanciful environment. In the Alhambra nothing seems more reasonable than those never-ending duels in which, for a lady's favour, gallant knights gave one another such blows that the air rang with them, such wounds that the ground was red with blood; but at sunset they separated and bound up their wounds and returned to the palace. And the king, at the relation of the adventure, was filled with amazement and with great content.

Yet, notwithstanding, I find in the Alhambra something unsatisfying; for many an inferior piece of architecture has set my mind a-working so that I have dreamed charming dreams, or seen vividly the life of other times. But here, I know not why, my imagination helps me scarcely at all. The existence led within these gorgeous walls is too remote; there is but little to indicate the thoughts, the feelings, of these people, and one can take the Alhambra only as a thing of beauty, and despair to understand.

I know that it is useless to attempt with words to give an idea of these numerous chambers and courts. A string of superlatives can do no more than tire the reader, an exact description can only confuse; nor is the painter able to give more than a suggestion of the bewildering charm. The effect is too emotional to be conveyed from man to man, and each must feel it for himself. Charles V. called him unhappy who had lost such treasure—desgraciado el que tal perdio—and showed his own appreciation by demolishing a part to build a Renaissance palace for himself! It appears that kings have not received from heaven with their right divine to govern wrong the inestimable gift of good taste; and for them possibly it is fortunate, since when, perchance, a sovereign has the artistic temperament, a discerning people—cuts off his head.

XXXIV

Boabdil the Unlucky

He was indeed unhappy who lost such treasure. The plain of Granada smiles with luxuriant crops, a beautiful country, gay with a hundred colours, and in summer when the corn is ripe it burns with vivid gold. The sun shines with fiery rays from the blue sky, and from the snow-capped mountains cool breezes temper the heat.

But from his cradle Boabdil was unfortunate; soothsayers prophesied that his reign would see the downfall of the Moorish power, and his every step tended to that end. Never in human existence was more evident the mysterious power of the three sisters, the daughters of Night; the Fates had spun his destiny, they placed the pitfalls before his feet and closed his eyes that he might not see; they hid from him the way of escape. Allah Achbar! It was destiny. In no other way can be explained the madness which sped the victims of that tragedy to their ruin; for with the enemy at their very gates, the Muslims set up and displaced kings, plotted and counterplotted. Boabdil was twice deposed and twice regained the throne. Even when the Christian kingdoms had united to consume the remnant of Moorish sovereignty the Moors could not cease their quarrelling. Boabdil looked on with satisfaction while the territory of the rival claimant to his crown was wrested from him, and did not understand that his turn must inevitably follow. Verily, the gods, wishing to destroy him, had deranged his mind. It is a pitiful history of treachery and folly that was enacted while the Catholic Sovereigns devoured the pomegranate, seed by seed.

To me history, with its hopes bound to be frustrated and its useless efforts, sometimes is so terrible that I can hardly read. I feel myself like one who lives, knowing the inevitable future, and yet is powerless to help. I see the acts of the poor human puppets, and know the disaster that must follow. I wonder if the Calvinists ever realised the agony of that dark God of theirs, omniscient and yet so strangely weak, to whom the eternal majesty of heaven was insufficient to save the predestined from everlasting death.

On March 22, 1491, began the last siege of Granada.

Ferdinand marched his army into the plain and began to destroy the crops, taking one by one the surrounding towns. He made no attempt upon the city itself, and hostilities were confined to skirmishes beneath the walls and single combats between Christian knights and Muslim cavaliers, wherein on either side prodigies of valour were performed. Through the summer the Moors were able to get provisions from the Sierra Nevada, but when, with winter, the produce of the earth grew less and its conveyance more difficult, famine began to make itself felt. The Moors consoled themselves with the hope that the besieging army would retire with the cold weather, for such in those days was the rule of warfare; but Ferdinand was in earnest. When an accidental fire burned his camp, he built him a town of solid stone and mortar, which he named Santa Fè. It stands still, the only town in Spain wherein a Moorish foot has never trod. Then the Muslims understood at last that the Spaniard would never again leave that fruitful land.

And presently they began to talk of surrender; Spanish gold worked its way with Boabdil's councillors, and before winter was out the capitulation was signed.

On the second day of the new year the final scene of the tragedy was acted. Early in the morning, before break of day, Boabdil had sent his mother and his wife with the treasure to precede him to the Alpuxarras, in which district, by the conditions of the treaty, Ferdinand had assigned him a little kingdom. Himself had one more duty to perform, and at the prearranged hour he sallied forth with a wretched escort of fifty knights. On the Spanish side the night had been spent in joy and feasting; but how must Boabdil have spent his, thinking of the inevitable morrow? To him the hours must have sped like minutes. What must have been the agony of his last look at the Alhambra, that jewel of incalculable price? Mendoza, the cardinal, had been sent forward to occupy the palace, and Boabdil passed him on the hill.

Soon he reached Ferdinand, who was stationed near a mosque surrounded by all the glory of his Court, pennons flying, and knights in their magnificent array. Boabdil would have thrown himself from his horse in sign of homage to kiss the hand of the king of Arragon, but Ferdinand prevented him. Then Boabdil delivered the keys of the Alhambra to the victor, saying: 'They are thine, O king, since

Allah so decrees it; use thy success with clemency and moderation.'
Moving on sadly he saluted Isabella, and passed to rejoin his family;
the Christians processioned to the city with psalm-singing.

But when Boabdil was crossing the mountains he turned to look at
the city he had lost, and burst into tears.

'You do well,' said his mother, 'to weep like a woman for what you
could not defend like a man.'

'Alas!' he cried, 'when were woes ever equal to mine?'

It was not to be expected that the pious Kings of Castille and
Arragon would keep their word, and means were soon invented to
hound the wretched Boabdil from the principality they had granted.
He crossed to Africa, and settled in Fez, of which the Sultan was his
kinsman. It is pathetic to learn that there he built himself a palace in
imitation of the Alhambra. At last, after many years, he was killed in
an obscure battle fighting against the Sultan's rebels, and the Arab
historian finishes the account of him with these words: 'Wretched
man! who could lose his life in another's cause, though he dared not
die in his own! Such was the immutable decree of destiny. Blessed
be Allah, who exalteth and abaseth the kings of the earth according
to His divine will, in the fulfilment of which consists that eternal
justice which regulates all human affairs.'

In the day of El Makkary, the historian of the Moorish Empire,
Boabdil's descendants had so fallen that they were nothing but
common beggars, subsisting upon the charitable allowances made
to the poor from the funds of the mosques.

*One generation passeth away and another generation cometh: but
the earth abideth for ever.*

XXXV

Los Pobres

People say that in Granada the beggars are more importunate than in any other Spanish town, but throughout Andalusia their pertinacity and number are amazing. They are licensed by the State, and the brass badge they wear makes them demand alms almost as a right. It is curious to find that the Spaniard, who is by no means a charitable being, gives very often to beggars—perhaps from superstitious motives, thinking their prayers will be of service, or fearing the evil eye, which may punish a refusal. Begging is quite an honourable profession in Spain; mendicants are charitably termed the poor, and not besmirched, as in England, with an opprobrious name.

I have never seen so many beggars as in Andalusia; at every church door there will be a dozen, and they stand or sit at each street corner, halt, lame and blind. Every possible deformity is paraded to arouse charity. Some look as though their eyes had been torn out, and they glare at you with horrible bleeding sockets; most indeed are blind, and you seldom fail to hear their monotonous cry, sometimes naming the saint's day to attract particular persons: 'Alms for the love of God, for a poor blind man on this the day of St. John!' They stand from morning till night, motionless, with hand extended, repeating the words as the sound of footsteps tells them some one is approaching; and then, as a coin is put in their hands, say gracefully: 'Dios se lo pagara! God will repay you.'

In Spain you do not pass silently when a beggar demands alms, but pray his mercy for God's love to excuse you: 'Perdone Usted por el amor de Dios!' Or else you beseech God to protect him: 'Dios le ampare!' And the mendicant, coming to your gate, sometimes invokes the Immaculate Virgin.

'Ave Maria purissima!' he calls.

And you, tired of giving, reply: 'Y por siempre! And for ever.'

He passes on, satisfied with your answer, and rings at the next door.

It is not only in Burgos that Théophile Gautier might have admired the beggar's divine rags; everywhere they wrap their cloaks about them in the same magnificent fashion. The capa, I suppose, is the most graceful of all the garments of civilised man, and never more so than when it barely holds together, a mass of rags and patches, stained by the rain and bleached by the sun and wind. It hangs straight from the neck in big simple lines, or else is flung over one shoulder with a pompous wealth of folds.

There is a strange immobility about Andalusian beggars which recalls their Moorish ancestry. They remain for hours in the same attitude, without moving a muscle; and one I knew in Seville stood day after day, from early morning till midnight, with hand outstretched in the same rather crooked position, never saying a word, but merely trusting to the passer-by to notice. The variety is amazing, men and women and children; and Seville at fair-time, or when the foreigners are coming for Holy Week, is like an enormous hospital. Mendicants assail you on all sides, the legless dragging themselves on their hands, the halt running towards you with a crutch, the blind led by wife or child, the deaf and dumb, the idiotic. I remember a woman with dead eyes and a huge hydrocephalic head, who sat in a bath-chair by one of the cathedral doors, and whenever people passed, cried shrilly for money in a high, unnatural voice. Sometimes they protrude maimed limbs, feetless legs or arms without hands; they display loathsome wounds, horribly inflamed; every variety of disease is shown to extort a copper. And so much is it a recognised trade that they have their properties, as it were: one old man whose legs had been shot away, trotted through the narrow streets of Seville on a diminutive ass, driving it into the shop-doors to demand his mite. Then there are the children, the little boys and girls that Murillo painted, barely covered by filthy rags, cherubs with black hair and shining eyes, the most importunate of all the tribe. The refusal of a halfpenny is followed impudently by demands for a cigarette, and as a last resort for a match; they wander about with keen eyes for cigar-ends, and no shred of a smoked leaf is too diminutive for them to get no further use from it.

And beside all these are the blind fiddlers, scraping out old-fashioned tunes that were popular thirty years ago; the guitarists, singing the flamenco songs which have been sung in Spain ever since the Moorish days; the buffoons, who extract tunes from a broomstick; the owners of performing dogs.

They are a picturesque lot, neither vicious nor ill-humoured. Begging is a fairly profitable trade, and not a very hard one; in winter el pobre can always find a little sunshine, and in summer a little shade. It is no hardship for him to sit still all day; he would probably do little else if he were a millionaire. He looks upon life without bitterness; Fate has not been very kind, but it is certainly better to be a live beggar than a dead king, and things might have been ten thousand times worse. For instance, he might not have been born a Spaniard, and every man in his senses knows that Spain is the greatest nation on earth, while to be born a citizen of some other country is the most dreadful misfortune that can befall him. He has his licence from the State, and a charitable public sees that he does not absolutely starve; he has cigarettes to smoke—to say that a blind man cannot enjoy tobacco is evidently absurd—and therefore, all these things being so, why should he think life such a woeful matter? While it lasts the sun is there to shine equally on rich and poor, and afterwards will not a paternal government find a grave in the public cemetery? It is true that the beggar shares it with quite a number of worthy persons, doubtless most estimable corpses, and his coffin even is but a temporary convenience—but still, what does it matter?

XXXVI

The Song

But the Moorish influence is nowhere more apparent than in the Spanish singing. There is nothing European in that quavering lament, in those long-drawn and monotonous notes, in those weird trills. The sounds are strange to the ear accustomed to less barbarous harmonies, and at first no melody is perceived; it is custom alone which teaches the sad and passionate charm of these things. A malagueña is the particular complaint of the maid sorrowing for an absent lover, of the peasant who ploughs his field in the declining day. The long notes of such a song, floating across the silence of the night, are like a new melody on the great harpsichord of human sorrow. No emotion is more poignant than that given by the faint sad sounds of a Spanish song as one wanders through the deserted streets in the dead of night; or far in the country, with the sun setting red in the cloudless sky, when the stillness is broken only by the melancholy chanting of a shepherd among the olive-trees.

An heritage of Moordom is the Spanish love for the improvisation of well-turned couplets; in olden days a skilful verse might procure the poet a dress of cloth-of-gold, and it did on one occasion actually raise a beggar-maid to a royal throne: even now it has power to secure the lover his lady's most tender smiles, or at the worst a glass of Manzanilla. The richness of the language helps him with his rhymes, and his southern imagination gives him manifold subjects. But, being the result of improvisation—no lady fair would consider the suit of a gallant who could not address her in couplets of his own devising—the Spanish song has a peculiar character. The various stanzas have no bearing upon one another; they consist of four or seven lines, but in either case each contains its definite sentiment; so that one verse may be a complete song, or the singer may continue as long as the muse prompts and his subject's charms occasion. The Spanish song is like a barbaric necklace in which all manner of different stones are strung upon a single cord, without thought for their mutual congruity.

Naturally the vast majority of the innumerable couplets thus invented are forgotten as soon as sung, but now and then the fortuitous excellence of one impresses it on the maker's recollection, and it may be preserved. Here is an example which has been agreeably translated by Mr. J. W. Crombie; but neither original nor English rendering can give an adequate idea of the charm which depends on the oriental melancholy of the music:

> Dos besos tengo en el alma
> Que no se apartan de mí:
> El ultimo de mi madre,
> Y el primero que te di.

> *Deep in my soul two kisses rest,*
> *Forgot they ne'er shall be:*
> *The last my mother's lips impressed,*
> *The first I stole from thee.*

Here is another, the survival of which testifies to the Spanish extreme love of a compliment; and the somewhat hackneyed sentiment can only have made it more pleasant to the feminine ear:

> Salga el sol, si ha de salir,
> Y si no, que nunca salga;
> Que para alumbrarme á mí
> La luz de tus ojos basta.

> *If the sun care to rise, let him rise,*
> *But if not, let him ever lie hid;*
> *For the light from my lady-love's eyes*
> *Shines forth as the sun never did.*

It is a diverting spectacle to watch a professional improviser in the throes of inspiration. This is one of the stock 'turns' of the Spanish music-hall, and one of the most popular. I saw a woman in Granada, who was quite a celebrity; and the barbaric wildness of her performance, with its accompaniment of hand-clapping, discordant cries, and twanging of guitar, harmonised well with my impression of the sombre and mediæval city.

She threaded her way to the stage among the crowded tables, through the auditorium, a sallow-faced creature, obese and large-boned, with coarse features and singularly ropy hair. She was accompanied by a fat small man with a guitar and a woman of mature age and ample proportions: it appeared that the cultivation of the muse, evidently more profitable than in England, conduced to adiposity. They stepped on the stage, taking chairs with them, for in Spain you do not stand to sing, and were greeted with plentiful applause. The little fat man began to play the long prelude to the couplet; the old woman clapped her hands and occasionally uttered a raucous cry. The poetess gazed into the air for inspiration. The guitarist twanged on, and in the audience there were scattered cries of Ole! Her companions began to look at the singer anxiously, for the muse was somewhat slow; and she patted her knee and groaned; at last she gave a little start and smiled. Ole! Ole! The inspiration had come. She gave a moan, which lengthened into the characteristic trill, and then began the couplet, beating time with her hands. Such an one as this:

Suspires que de mí salgan,
Y otros que de tí saldran,
Si en el camino se encuentran
Que de cosas se diran!

If all the sighs thy lips now shape
Could meet upon the way
With those that from mine own escape
What things they'd have to say!

She finished, and all three rose from their chairs and withdrew them, but it was only a false exit; immediately the applause grew clamorous they sat down again, and the little fat man repeated his introduction.

But this time there was no waiting. The singer had noticed a well-known bull-fighter and quickly rolled off a couplet in his praise. The subject beamed with delight, and the general enthusiasm knew no bounds. The people excitedly threw their hats on the stage, and these were followed by a shower of coppers, which the performers, more heedful to the compensation of Art than to its dignity, grovelled to picked up.

Here is a lover's praise of the whiteness of his lady's skin:

> La neve por tu cara
> Paso diciendo:
> En donde no hago falta
> No me detengo.

> *Before thy brow the snow-flakes*
> *Hurry past and say:*
> *'Where we are not needed,*
> *Wherefore should we stay?'*

And this last, like the preceding translated by Mr. Crombie, shows once more how characteristic are Murillo's Holy Families of the popular sentiment:

> La Virgen lava la ropa,
> San José la esta tendiendo,
> Santa Ana entretiene el niño,
> Y el agua se va riendo.

> *The Virgin is washing the clothes at the brook.*
> *And Saint Joseph hangs them to dry.*
> *Saint Anna plays with the Holy Babe,*
> *And the water flows smiling by.*

XXXVII

Jerez

Jerez is the Andalusian sunshine again after the dark clouds of Granada. It is a little town in the middle of a fertile plain, clean and comfortable and spacious. It is one of the richest places in Spain; the houses have an opulent look, and without the help of Baedeker you may guess that they contain respectable persons with incomes, and carriages and horses, with frock-coats and gold watch-chains. I like the people of Jerez; their habitual expression suggests a consciousness that the Almighty is pleased with them, and they without doubt are well content with the Almighty. The main street, with its trim shops and its cafés, has the air of a French provincial town—an appearance of agreeable ease and dulness.

Every building in Jerez is washed with lime, and in the sunlight the brilliancy is dazzling. You realise then that in Seville the houses are not white—although the general impression is of a white town—but, on the contrary, tinted with various colours from faintest pink to pale blue, pale green; they remind you of the summer dresses of women. The soft tones are all mingled with the sunlight and very restful. But Jerez is like a white banner floating under the cloudless sky, the pure white banner of Bacchus raised defiantly against the gaudy dyes of teetotalism and its shrieking trumpets.

Jerez the White is, of course, the home of sherry, and the whole town is given over to the preparation of the grateful juice. The air is impregnated with a rich smell. The sun shines down on Jerez; and its cleanliness, its prosperity, are a rebuke to harsh-voiced contemners of the grape.

You pass bodega after bodega, cask-factories, bottle-factories. A bottle-factory is a curious, interesting place, an immense barn, sombre, so that the eye loses itself in the shadows of the roof; and the scanty light is red and lurid from the furnaces, which roar hoarsely and long. Against the glow the figures of men, half-naked, move silently, performing the actions of their craft with a monotonous regularity which is strange and solemn. They move to and fro, carrying an iron instrument on which is the molten mass of red-hot glass, and it gleams with an extraordinary warm brilliancy. It twists hither and thither in obedience to the artisan's deft movements; it coils and writhes into odd shapes, like a fire-snake curling in the torture of its own unearthly ardour. The men pass so regularly, with such a silent and exact precision, that it seems a weird and mystic measure they perform—a rhythmic dance of unimaginable intricacy, whose meaning you cannot gather and whose harmony escapes you. The flames leap and soar in a thousand savage forms, and their dull thunder fills your ears with a confusion of sound. Your eyes become accustomed to the dimness, and you discern more clearly the features of those swarthy men, bearded and gnome-like. But the molten mass has been put into the mould; you watch it withdrawn, the bottom indented, the mouth cut and shaped. And now it is complete, but still red-hot, and glowing with an infernal transparency, gem-like and wonderful; it is a bottle fit now for the juice of satanic vineyards, and the miraculous potions of eternal youth, for which men in the old days bartered their immortal souls.

And the effect of a bodega is picturesque, too, though in a different way. It is a bright and cheerful spot, a huge shed with whitewashed walls and an open roof supported by dark beams; great casks are piled up, impressing you in their vast rotundity with a sort of aldermanic stateliness. The whole place is fragrant with clean, vinous perfumes. Your guide carries a glass and a long filler. You taste wine after wine, in different shades of brown; light wines to drink with your dinner, older wines to drink before your coffee; wines more than a century old, of which the odour is more delicate than violets; new wines of the preceding year, strong and rough; Amontillados, with the softest flavour in the world; Manzanillas for the gouty; Marsalas, heavy and sweet; wines that smell of wild-flowers; cheap wines and expensive wines. Then the brandies—the distiller tells you proudly that Spanish brandy is made from wine, and contemptuously that French brandy is not—old brandies for which a toper would sell his soul; new brandies like fusel-oil; brandies mellow and mild and rich. It is a drunkard's paradise.

And why should not the drinker have his paradise? The teetotallers have slapped their bosoms and vowed that liquor was the devil's own invention. (Note, by the way, that liquor is a noble word that should not be applied to those weak-kneed abominations that insolently flaunt their lack of alcohol. Let them be called liquids or fluids or beverages, or what you will. Liquor is a word for heroes, for the British tar who has built up British glory—Imperialism is quite the fashion now.) And for a hundred years none has dared lift his voice in refutation of these dyspeptic slanders. The toper did not care, he nursed his bottle and let the world say what it would; but the moderate drinker was abashed. Who will venture to say that a glass of beer gives savour to the humblest crust, and comforts Corydon, lamenting the inconstancy of Phyllis? Who will come forward and strike an attitude and prove the benefits of the grape? (The attitude is essential, for without it you cannot hope to impress your fellow men.) Rise up in your might, ye lovers of hop and grape and rye—rise up and slay the Egyptians. Be honest and thank your stars for the cup that cheers. Bacchus was not a pot-bellied old sot, but a beautiful youth with vine-leaves in his hair, Bacchus the lover of flowers; and Ariadne was charming.

The country about Jerez undulates in just such an easy comfortable fashion as you would expect. It is scenery of the gentlest and pleasantest type, sinuous; little hills rising with rounded lines and fertile valleys. The vines cover the whole land, creeping over the brown soil fantastically, black stumps, shrivelled and gnarled, tortured into uncouth shapes; they remind you of the creeping things in a naturalist's museum, of giant spiders and great dried centipedes and scorpions. But imagine the vineyards later, when the spring has stirred the earth with fecundity! The green shoots tenderly forth; at first it is all too delicate for a colour, it is but a mist of indescribable tenuity; and gradually the leaves burst out and trail along the ground with ever-increasing luxuriance; and then it is a rippling sea of passionate verdure.

But I liked Jerez best towards evening, when the sun had set and the twilight glided through the tortuous alleys like a woman dressed in white. Then, as I walked in the silent streets, narrow and steep, with their cobble-paving, the white houses gained a new aspect. There seemed not a soul in the world, and the loneliness was more intoxicating than all their wines; the shining sun was gone, and the sky lost its blue richness, it became so pale that you felt it like a face of death—and the houses looked like long rows of tombs. We walked through the deserted streets, I and the woman dressed in white, side by side silently; our footsteps made no sound upon the stones. And Jerez was wrapped in a ghostly shroud. Ah, the beautiful things I have seen which other men have not!

XXXVIII

Cadiz

I admire the strenuous tourist who sets out in the morning with his well-thumbed Baedeker to examine the curiosities of a foreign town, but I do not follow in his steps; his eagerness after knowledge, his devotion to duty, compel my respect, but excite me to no imitation. I prefer to wander in old streets at random without a guide-book, trusting that fortune will bring me across things worth seeing; and if occasionally I miss some monument that is world-famous, more often I discover some little dainty piece of architecture, some scrap of decoration, that repays me for all else I lose. And in this fashion the less pretentious beauties of a town delight me, which, if I sought under the guidance of the industrious German, would seem perhaps scarcely worth the trouble. Nor do I know that there is in Cadiz much to attract the traveller beyond the grace with which it lies along the blue sea and the unstudied charm of its gardens, streets, and market-place; the echo in the cathedral to which the gaping tripper listens with astonishment leaves me unmoved; and in the church of Santa Catalina, which contains the last work of Murillo, upon which he was engaged at his death, I am more interested in the tall stout priest, unctuous and astute, who shows me his treasure, than in the picture itself. I am relieved now and again to visit a place that has no obvious claims on my admiration; it throws me back on the peculiarities of the people, on the stray incidents of the street, on the contents of the shops.

Cadiz is said to be the gayest town in Andalusia. Spaniards have always a certain gravity; they are not very talkative, and like the English, take their pleasures a little sadly. But here lightness of heart is thought to reign supreme, and the inhabitants have not even the apparent seriousness with which the Sevillan cloaks a somewhat vacant mind. They are great theatre-goers, and as dancers, of course, have been famous since the world began. But I doubt whether Cadiz deserves its reputation, for it always seems to me a little prim. The streets are well-kept and spacious, the houses, taller than is usual in Andalusia, have almost as cared-for an appearance as those in a prosperous suburb of London; and it is only quite occasionally, when you catch a glimpse of tawny rock and of white breakwater against the blue sea, that by a reminiscence of Naples you can persuade yourself it is as immoral as they say. For, not unlike the Syren City, Cadiz lies white and cool along the bay, with gardens at the water's edge; but it has not the magic colour of its rival, it is quieter, smaller, more restful; and on the whole lacks that agreeable air of wickedness which the Italian town possesses to perfection. It is impossible to be a day in Naples without discovering that it is the most depraved city in Europe; there is something in the atmosphere which relaxes the moral fibre, and the churchwarden who keeps guard in the bosom of every Englishman falls asleep, so that you feel capable of committing far more than the seven deadly sins. Of course, you don't, but still it is comfortable to have them within reach.

I came across, while examining the wares of a vendor of antiquities, a contemporary narrative from the Spanish side of the attack made on Cadiz by Sir Francis Drake when he set out to singe the beard of Philip II.; and this induced me afterwards to look into the English story. It is far from me to wish to inform the reader, but the account is not undiverting, and shows, besides, a frame of mind which the Anglo-Saxon has not ceased to cultivate. 'But the Almighty God,' says the historian, 'knowing and seeing his (the Spanish king's) wicked intent to punish, molest, and trouble His little flock, the children of Israel, hath raised up a faithful Moses for the defence of His chosen, and will not suffer His people utterly to fall into the hands of their enemies.' Drake set sail from Plymouth with four of her Majesty's ships, two pinnaces, and some twenty merchantmen. A vessel was sent after, charging him not to show hostilities, but the messenger, owing to contrary winds, could never come near the admiral, and vastly to the annoyance of the Virgin Queen, as she solemnly assured the ambassadors of foreign powers, had to sail home. Under the circumstances it was, perhaps, hardly discreet of her to take so large a share of the booty.

Faithful Moses arrived in Cadiz, spreading horrid consternation, and the Spanish pamphlet shows very vividly the confusion of the enemy. It appears that, had he boldly landed, he might have sacked the town, but he imagined the preparations much greater than they were. However, he was not idle. 'The same night our general, having, by God's good favour and sufferance, opportunity to punish the enemy of God's true gospel and our daily adversary, and further willing to discharge his expected duty towards God, his peace and country, began to sink and fire divers of their ships.'

The English fleet burned thirty sail of great burden, and captured vast quantities of the bread, wheat, wine and oil which had been prepared for the descent upon England. Sir Francis Drake himself remarks that 'the sight of the terrible fires were to us very pleasant, and mitigated the burden of our continual travail, wherein we were busied for two nights and one day, in discharging, firing, and lading of provisions.'

It is a curious thing to see entirely deserted a place of entertainment, where great numbers of people are in the habit of assembling. A theatre by day, without a soul in it, gives me always a sensation of the ridiculous futility of things; and a public garden towards evening offers the same emotion. On the morrow I was starting for Africa; I watched the sunset from the quays of Cadiz, the vapours of the twilight rise and envelop the ships in greyness, and I walked by the alamadas that stretch along the bay till I came to the park. The light was rapidly failing and I found myself alone. It had quaint avenues of short palms, evidently not long planted, and between them rows of yellow iron chairs arranged with great neatness and precision. It was there that on Sunday I had seen the populace disport itself, and it was full of life then, gay and insouciant. The fair ladies drove in their carriages, and the fine gentlemen, proud of their English clothes, lounged idly. The chairs were taken by all the lesser fry, by stout mothers, dragons attendant on dark-eyed girls, and their lovers in broad hats, in all the gala array of the flamenco. There was a joyous clamour of speech and laughter; the voices of Spanish women are harsh and unrestrained; the park sparkled with colour, and the sun caught the fluttering of countless fans.

For those blithe people it seemed that there was no morrow: the present was there to be enjoyed, divine and various, and the world was full of beauty and of sunshine; merely to live was happiness enough; if there was pain or sorrow it served but to enhance the gladness. The hurrying hours for a while had ceased their journey. Life was a cup of red wine, and they were willing to drink its very dregs, a brimming cup in which there was no bitterness, but a joy more thrilling than the gods could give in all their paradise.

But now I walked alone between the even rows of chairs. The little palms were so precise, with their careful foliage, that they did not look like real trees; the flower-beds were very stiff and neat, and now and then a pine stood out, erect and formal as if it were a cardboard tree from a Noah's Ark. The scene was so artificial that it brought to my mind the setting of a pantomime. I stopped, almost expecting a thousand ballet-girls to appear from the wings, scantily clad, and go through a measure to the playing of some sudden band, and retire and come forward till the stage was filled and a great tableau formed.

But the day grew quite dim, and the vast stage remained empty. The painted scene became still more unreal, and presently the park was filled with the ghostly shapes of all the light-hearted people who had lived their hour and exhibited their youth in the empty garden. I heard the whispered compliments, and the soft laughter of the ladies; there was a peculiar little snap as gaily they closed their fans.

XXXIX

El Genero Chico

In the evening I wandered again along the quay, my thoughts part occupied with the novel things I expected from Morocco, part sorrowful because I must leave the scented land of Spain. I seemed never before to have enjoyed so intensely the exquisite softness of the air, and there was all about me a sense of spaciousness which gave a curious feeling of power. In the harbour, on the ships, the lights of the masts twinkled like the stars above; and looking over the stony parapet, I heard the waves lap against the granite like a long murmur of regret; I tried to pierce the darkness, straining my eyes to see some deeper obscurity which I might imagine to be the massive coasts of Africa. But at last I could bear the solitude no longer, and I dived into the labyrinth of streets.

At first, in unfrequented ways, I passed people only one by one, some woman walking rapidly with averted face, or a pair of chattering students; but as I came near the centre of the town the passers-by grew more frequent, and suddenly I found myself in the midst of a thronging, noisy crowd. I looked up and saw that I was opposite a theatre; the people had just come from the second funcion. I had heard that the natives of Cadiz were eager theatre-goers, and was curious to see how they took this pleasure. I saw also that the next piece was Las Borrachos, a play of Seville life that I had often seen; and I felt that I could not spend my last evening better than in living again some of those scenes which pattered across my heart now like little sorrowful feet.

The theatre in Spain is the only thing that has developed further than in the rest of Europe—in fact, it has nearly developed clean away. The Spaniards were the first to confess that dramatic art bored them to death; and their habits rendered impossible the long play which took an evening to produce. Eating late, they did not wish to go to the theatre till past nine; being somewhat frivolous, they could not sit for more than an hour without going outside and talking to their friends; and they were poor. To satisfy their needs the genero chico, or little style, sprang into existence; and quickly every theatre in Spain was given over to the system of four houses a night. Each function is different, and the stall costs little more than sixpence.

We English are idealists; and on the stage especially reality stinks in our nostrils. The poor are vulgar, and in our franker moments we confess our wish to have nothing to do with them. The middle classes are sordid; we have enough of them in real life, and no desire to observe their doings at the theatre, particularly when we wear our evening clothes. But when a dramatist presents duchesses to our admiring eyes, we feel at last in our element; we watch the acts of persons whom we would willingly meet at dinner, and our craving for the ideal is satisfied.

But in Spain nobles are common and excite no overwhelming awe. The Spaniard, most democratic of Europeans, clamours for realism, and nothing pleases him more than a literal transcript of the life about him. The manners and customs of good society do not entertain him, and the genero chico concerns itself almost exclusively with the lower classes. The bull-fighter is, of course, one of the most usual figures; and round him are gathered the lovers of the ring, inn-keepers, cobblers and carpenters, policemen, workmen, flower-sellers, street-singers, cigarette girls, country maidens. The little pieces are innumerable, and together form a compend of low life in Spain; the best are full of gaiety and high spirits, with a delicate feeling for character, and often enough are touched by a breath of poetry. Songs and dances are introduced, and these come in the more naturally since the action generally takes place on a holiday. The result is a musical comedy in one act; but with nothing in it of the entertainment which is a joy to the British public: an Andalusian audience would never stand that representation of an impossible and vulgar world in which the women are all trollops and the men, rips, nincompoops and bounders; they would never suffer the coarse humour and the shoddy patriotism.

Unfortunately, these one-act plays have destroyed the legitimate drama. Whereas Maria Guerrero, that charming actress, will have a run of twenty nights in a new play by Echegaray, a popular zarzuela will be acted hundreds of times in every town in Spain. But none can regret that the Spaniards have evolved these very national little pieces, and little has been lost in the non-existence of an indefinite number of imitations from the French. The zarzuela, I should add, lasts about an hour, and for the most part is divided into three scenes.

Such a play as Los Borrachos is nothing less than a genre picture of Seville life. It reminds one of a painting by Teniers; and I should like to give some idea of it, since it is really one of the best examples of the class, witty, varied, and vivacious. But an obstacle presents itself in the fact that I can find no vestige of a plot. The authors set out to characterise the various lovers of the vine, (nowhere in Andalusia are the devotees of the yellow Manzanilla more numerous than in Seville,) and with telling strokes have drawn the good-natured tippler, the surly tippler, the religious tippler. To these they have added other types, which every Andalusian can recognise as old friends—the sharp-tongued harridan, the improviser of couplets with his ridiculous vanity, the flower-seller, and the 'prentice-boy of fifteen, who, notwithstanding his tender years, is afflicted with love for the dark-eyed heroine. The action takes place first in a street, then in a court-yard, lastly in a carpenter's shop. There are dainty love-scenes between Soledad, the distressed maiden, and Juanillo, the flower-seller; and one, very Spanish, where the witty and precocious apprentice offers her his diminutive hand and heart. Numerous people come and go, the drunkards drink and quarrel and make peace; the whole thing, if somewhat confused, is very life-like, and runs with admirable lightness and ease. It is true that the play has neither beginning nor end, but perhaps that only makes it seem the truer; and if the scenes have no obvious connection they are all amusing and characteristic. It is acted with extraordinary spirit. The players, indeed, are not acting, but living their ordinary lives, and it is pleasant to see the zest with which they throw themselves into the performance. When the hero presses the heroine in his arms, smiles and passionate glances pass between them, which suggest that even the love-making is not entirely make-believe.

I wish I could translate the song which Juanillo sings when he passes his lady's window, bearing his basket of flowers:

> Carnations for pretty girls that are true,
> Musk-roses for pretty girls that are coy,
> Rosebuds as small as thy mouth, my dearest,
> And roses as fair as thy cheeks.

134

I cannot, indeed, resist the temptation of giving one verse in that Andalusian dialect, from which all harsh consonants and unmusical sounds have been worn away—the most complete and perfect language in the world for lovers and the passion of love:

Sal, morena, á tu ventana,
Mira las flores que traigo;
Sal y di si son bastantes
Pa arfombrita de tu cuarto.
Que yo te quiero
Y a ti te doy
Tos los tesoros der mundo entero,
To le que vargo, to lo que soy.

XL

Adios

And then the morrow was come. Getting up at five to catch my boat, I went down to the harbour; a grey mist hung over the sea, and the sun had barely risen, a pallid, yellow circle; the fishing-boats lolled on the smooth, dim water, and fishermen in little groups blew on their fingers.

And from Cadiz I saw the shores of Spain sink into the sea; I saw my last of Andalusia. Who, when he leaves a place that he has loved, can help wondering when he will see it again? I asked the wind, and it sighed back the Spanish answer: 'Quien sabe? Who knows?' The traveller makes up his mind to return quickly, but all manner of things happen, and one accident or another prevents him; time passes till the desire is lost, and when at last he comes back, himself has altered or changes have occurred in the old places and all seems different. He looks quite coldly at what had given an intense emotion, and though he may see new things, the others hardly move him; it is not thus he imagined them in the years of waiting. And how can he tell what the future may have in store; perhaps, notwithstanding all his passionate desires, he will indeed never return.

Of course the intention of this book is not to induce people to go to Spain: railway journeys are long and tedious, the trains crawl, and the hotels are bad. Experienced globe-trotters have told me that all mountains are very much alike, and that pictures, when you have seen a great many, offer no vast difference. It is much better to read books of travel than to travel oneself; he really enjoys foreign lands who never goes abroad; and the man who stays at home, preserving his illusions, has certainly the best of it. How delightful is the anticipation as he looks over time-tables and books of photographs, forming delightful images of future pleasure! But the reality is full of disappointment, and the more famous the monument the bitterer the disillusion. Has any one seen St. Peter's without asking himself: Is that all? And the truest enjoyment arises from things that come unexpectedly, that one had never heard of. Then, living in a strange land, one loses all impression of its strangeness; it is only afterwards, in England, that one realises the charm and longs to return; and a hundred pictures rise to fill the mind with delight. Why can one not be strong enough to leave it at that and never tempt the fates again?

The wisest thing is to leave unvisited in every country some place that one wants very much to see. In Italy I have never been to Siena, and in Andalusia I have taken pains to avoid Malaga. The guide-books tell me there is nothing whatever to see there; and according to them it is merely a prosperous sea-port with a good climate. But to me, who have never seen it, Malaga is something very different; it is the very cream of Andalusia, where every trait and characteristic is refined to perfect expression.

I imagine Malaga to be the most smiling town on the seaboard, and it lies along the shore ten times more charmingly than Cadiz. The houses are white, whiter than in Jerez; the patios are beautiful with oranges and palm-trees, and the dark green of the luxuriant foliage contrasts with the snowy walls. In Malaga the sky is always blue and the sun shines, but the narrow Arab streets are cool and shady. The passionate odours of Andalusia float in the air, the perfume of a myriad cigarettes and the fresh scent of fruit and flower. The blue sea lazily kisses the beach and fishing-boats bask on its bosom.

In Malaga, for me, there are dark churches, with massive, tall pillars; the light falls softly through the painted glass, regilding the golden woodwork, the angels and the saints and the bishops in their mitres. The air is heavy with incense, and women in mantillas kneel in the half-light, praying silently. Now and then I come across an old house with a fragment of Moorish work, reminding me that here again the Moors have left their mark.

And in Malaga, for me, the women are more lovely than in Seville; for their dark eyes glitter marvellously, and their lips, so red and soft, are ever trembling with a half-formed smile. They are more graceful than the daffodils, their hands are lovers' sighs, and their voice is a caressing song. (What was your voice like, Rosarito? Alas! it is so long ago that I forget.) The men are tall and slender, with strong, clear features and shining eyes, deep sunken in their sockets.

In Malaga, for me, life is a holiday in which there are no dullards and no bores; all the world is strong and young and full of health, and there is nothing to remind one of horrible things. Malaga, I know, is the most delightful place in Andalusia. Oh, how refreshing it is to get away from sober fact, but what a fool I should be ever to go there!

The steamer plods on against the wind slowly, and as the land sinks away, unsatisfied to leave the impressions hovering vaguely through my mind, I try to find the moral. The Englishman, ever somewhat sententiously inclined, asks what a place can teach him. The churchwarden in his bosom gives no constant, enduring peace; and after all, though he may be often ridiculous, it is the churchwarden who has made good part of England's greatness.

And most obviously Andalusia suggests that it might not be ill to take things a little more easily: we English look upon life so very seriously, so much without humour. Is it worth while to be quite so strenuous? At the stations on the line between Jerez and Cadiz, I noticed again how calmly they took things; people lounged idly talking to one another; the officials of the railway smoked their cigarettes; no one was in a hurry, time was long, and whether the train arrived late or punctual could really matter much to no one. A beggar came to the window, a cigarette-end between his lips.

'Caballero! Alms for the love of God for a poor old man. God will repay you!'

He passed slowly down the train. It waited for no reason; the passengers stared idly at the loungers on the platform, and they stared idly back. No one moved except to roll himself a cigarette. The sky was blue and the air warm and comforting. Life seemed good enough, and above all things easy. There was no particular cause to trouble. What is the use of hurrying to pile up money when one can live on so little? What is the use of reading these endless books? Why not let things slide a little, and just take what comes our way? It is only for a little while, and then the great antique mother receives us once more in her bosom. And there are so many people in the world. Think again of all the countless hordes who have come and gone, and who will come and go; the immense sea of Time covers them, and what matters the life they led? What odds is it that they ever existed at all? Let us do our best to be happy; the earth is good and sweet-smelling, there is sunshine and colour and youth and loveliness; and afterwards—well, let us shrug our shoulders and not think of it.

And then in bitter irony, contradicting my moral, a train came in with a number of Cuban soldiers. There were above fifty of them, and they had to change at the junction. They reached out to open the carriage doors and crawled down to the platform. Some of them seemed at death's door; they could not walk, and chairs were brought that they might be carried; others leaned heavily on their companions. And they were dishevelled, with stubbly beards. But what struck me most was the deathly colour; for their faces were almost green, while round their sunken eyes were great white rings, and the white was ghastly, corpse-like. They trooped along in a dazed and listless fashion, wasted with fever, and now and then one stopped, shaken with a racking cough; he leaned against the wall, and put his hand to his heart as if the pain were unendurable. It was a pitiful sight. They were stunted and under-sized; they ceased to develop when they went to the cruel island, and they were puny creatures with hollow chests and thin powerless limbs; often, strangely enough, their faces had remained quite boyish. They were twenty or twenty-two, and they looked sixteen. And then, by the sight of those boys who had never known youth with its joyful flowers, doomed to a hopeless life, I was forced against my will to another moral. Perhaps some would recover, but the majority must drag on with ruined health, fever-stricken, dying one by one, falling like the unripe fruit of a rotten tree. They had no chance, poor wretches! They would return to their miserable homes; they could not work, and their people were too poor to keep them—so they must starve. Their lives were even shorter than those of the rest, and what pleasure had they had?

And that is the result of the Spanish insouciance—death and corruption, loss of power and land and honour, the ruin of countless lives, and absolute decay. It is rather a bitter irony, isn't it? And now all they have left is their sunshine and the equanimity which nothing can disturb.

www.ingramcontent.com/pod-product-compliance
Lightning Source LLC
Chambersburg PA
CBHW020141180626
46810CB00004B/1673